D1366932

MAN RAY

FAY RAY mated with Arco

Number Nine | Art | Ken | Blaise | Glenn | Speedy | CROOKY | CHUNDO | BATTINA

CROOKY mated with Unknown dog

CROOKY mated with Val

BATTY mated with Ferdinand

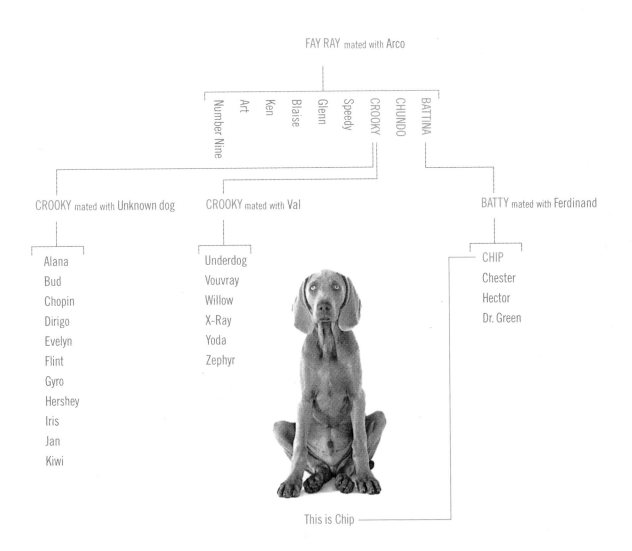

Alana
Bud
Chopin
Dirigo
Evelyn
Flint
Gyro
Hershey
Iris
Jan
Kiwi

Underdog
Vouvray
Willow
X-Ray
Yoda
Zephyr

CHIP
Chester
Hector
Dr. Green

This is Chip

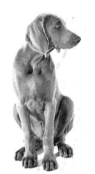

WILLIAM WEGMAN

PUPPIES

HYPERION

WILLIAM WEGMAN

PUPPIES

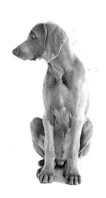

NEW YORK

Dedicated to Fay

I didn't really want a

dog.

I was too busy being an artist. But my wife did, so I promised her that when we got to California we would get one. I was hoping she would forget. It was a long drive to Los Angeles from Madison, where I had been teaching in the art department of the University of Wisconsin, but she didn't forget. When we arrived we decided to look for a dalmatian. We couldn't find one. Apparently there was a dalmatian shortage in 1970. Someone said weimaraners were good dogs. I had never heard of them.

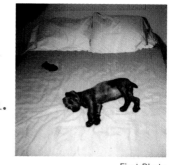

First Photo

We chose our six-week-old weimaraner puppy from a litter in Long Beach, California. Sitting there in the dining room in a ray of light, he looked like a little old man. Except for a big case of chewy-itis, there was nothing puppylike about him. I named him Man Ray.

The first thing I did when I got Man Ray home was to take his picture: on the bed, deep asleep, a sock on the bed near him. There was a similarity between this sock and Man Ray. Man Ray looked like the sock. The sock looked like Man Ray. Man Ray looked like many things. This idea grew on me.

But Man Ray had some problems. He followed me everywhere. *Everywhere.* Outside, inside, in the kitchen, to the bathroom, to the bedroom…and to the studio. I was constantly trying to quiet him, to keep him from emitting his annoying high-frequency whine. He was very clever at getting attention and he was starting to take over. Man Ray learned, for instance, that if he hovered over a glass coffee table with a boulder in his mouth, he would have your complete attention. Some of my students in the art department strongly suggested that I get rid of him. They could see what I couldn't: Man Ray was running the show.

Only in the studio, when I let him work with me, was Man Ray well behaved. No high-pitched whining there. He was calm and attentive while posing for pictures and performing in live video pieces. There was something reassuring to Man Ray about the ordeal of setting up the recording sessions with the video camera and the tape deck. I had a hard time getting things to work. Those early machines were much more clunky and demanding than current models. Setting up lights, props, and the stage, as well as the serious tone and the focus of it all, contributed to the high-mindedness of the endeavor. This stuff must be important to Bill, thought Man

Someone said weimaraners were good dogs. I had never heard of them.

Ray. Ray changed the way I thought about my work. I became more and more attached to him.

In his eleventh year, Man Ray became gravely ill. One day he suddenly collapsed during a walk. It turned out he had pancreatic cancer. I thought that I could prepare for the inevitable by looking it straight on. The large format Polaroids from that year, which include Dusted and the life-size portrait heads of Man Ray, are to me the most profound works our photographic relationship summoned. Some are portraits of a dear friend, others are more like posthumous commemoratives. However, this work would not prepare me for the loss I was to experience. Man Ray died in 1982, late in his eleventh year. I was devastated. I vowed that I would never get another dog.

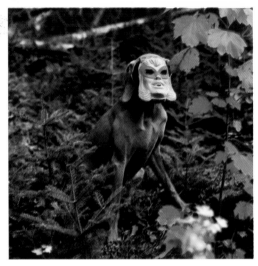

Wonder Woman

I didn't know Fay Ray as a puppy. She was six months old and almost fully grown when I met her in April 1986, in Memphis, Tennessee, five years after Man Ray's death. I had just given a slide lecture about my work to students at Memphis State. A woman in the audience came up to me and said she loved my pictures of Man Ray. She bred weimaraners and offered me one of her puppies. *"I'm not going to get another dog,"* I said. *"How about tomorrow,"* she replied. *"Just for a visit…"*

A month later, a weimaraner puppy was on my bed in New York City. What a beauty! Cinnamon Girl, as she was called, had a beautiful body, feminine and strong. She looked like she had wandered out of a Rousseau painting. Those luminous yellow eyes. And she had a pedigree. I renamed her Fay. Fay Ray.

I had no interest in using Fay as a model. I had already done that with Man Ray. Of course I took Fay's picture, but only family snapshots, and then only a few times. One August day while in Maine, I took my photo equipment— tripod, meter, Hasselblad camera—and Fay down to a small stream not far from my cabin. I brought along a few props, including a Wonder Woman outfit. There, in the privacy of our own secluded sanctuary, I posed Fay on the bank of the brook and dressed her in the costume. She remained perfectly still while I set up my camera on the tripod, read the light meter, and composed the shot, a process that took more than a few minutes. I could see her peering intently through the holes in the mask. She looked happy and proud. It's about time, she seemed to say. Aren't you William Wegman, the dog photographer? The picture wasn't memorable, but the experience was affirming.

When we returned to New York in the fall, I began to work with Fay at the Polaroid 20 x 24 Studio with the camera I had been using since 1979, the very one I used during Man Ray's last three years. At first the session was kind of spooky.

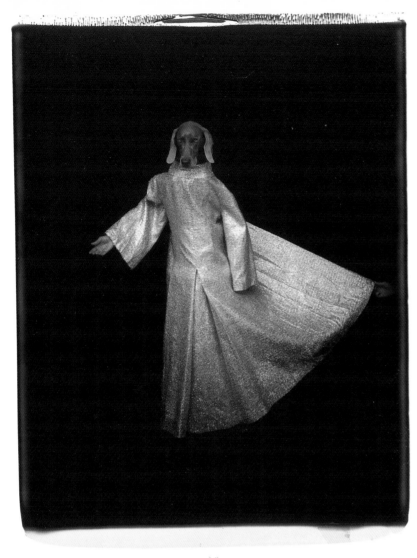

To me, Fay was
part Greta Garbo
and part
Joan Crawford.

I was haunted by the memory
of Man Ray. It wasn't until
I allowed myself to step back
and see how different Fay
was from Ray that I began to
lose my inhibitions. Fay was
young, vulnerable, feminine,
mysterious—a thoroughbred
beauty, and the way she
inhabited the picture was
strikingly different. Ray was
stoic, passive, noble, and
wise. Fay's yellow eyes lit
up a photograph and her
sculpted body graced it in
an altogether new way.

Once I started with Fay
I never stopped to question
our work together, and it really
took off. One day, I put Fay
on a stool to give the illusion
that she was tall. I dressed
her and gave her arms.
Actually they were my assistant Andrea's arms, long and
graceful. They fit her well.
Now Fay had hands to hold
things with. She had gestures
to go with her new tall look

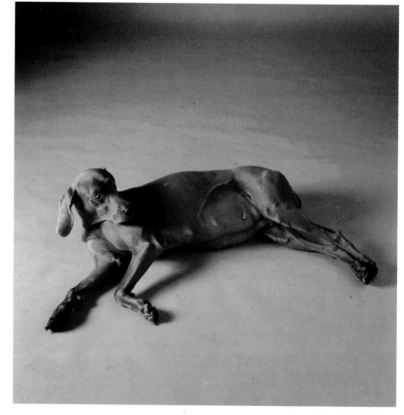

and her powerful gaze. Fay had become more Sarah Bernhardt than Lassie.

I got to know more about Fay through her puppies. When Fay turned four, I decided to breed her. Virginia Alexander, a well-known weimaraner expert, recommended we breed Fay to her dog Champion Laudenburg Arco von Reiteralm (also known as Arco), a German-born weimaraner male. First we had to get permission from the German Weimaraner Club. Had Fay won any shows? What championship rings had she collected? Any belts? Had she this or that certificate? We sent a resume of her museum shows and a list of the public and private collections in which she was represented to Germany, and this amused them enough to approve the breeding.

Fay pregnant was not the prettiest sight. She was usually such a sleek, elegant creature. I don't think she liked putting on weight. I wondered what kind of mother she would be to her puppies. Would she ignore them... pretend they weren't hers? I could see Fay behaving in that way. To me, Fay was part Greta Garbo and part Joan Crawford.

In anticipation of Fay giving birth, we left New York City and moved to my house in upstate New York. There are a lot of things to worry about when your loved one is expecting. I was sent the recommended whelping books by Virginia, and I started to build a whelping box. Normally a weimaraner's gestation period is 63 days. When the time is near, the dog's

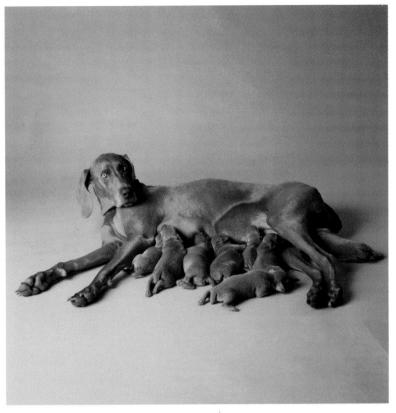

I wasn't exactly ready for this occasion.

As I was reading, Fay left the porch couch and made her way onto the living room couch, the sac with the tiny feet hanging about 1–3/4 inches out. It seemed to be stuck. I gave a careful pull and out slid Chundo. I recall saying, *"Oh, my God!"* five times during this event. I broke the membrane sac encasing his head. His eyes were closed, and he was completely still. The diagram on page 285 showed how to jump-start the newborn by using the swinging method. This was not easy. The sac was extremely slippery, but I managed to do as the book instructed twice…three times. Some fluid came out of his nose and then, suddenly, I heard a squeak! I beamed proudly and presented him to Fay. She began to care for

temperature will drop suddenly from the normal 101°–102°F to 97°–99°F. One of the books recommended that the dog's temperature be taken on the fifty-sixth day so that you can get absolutely, totally, and completely ready. I did. The thermometer read 97°F. I took it again: 96.08°F.

Fay was shivering and acting strangely. We were on the big couch, out on the porch. It was Sunday, June 10, 1989, at about 2 P.M. Suddenly, she hunched over. I looked at her behind and saw a gray-black rubber balloon nesting there. No, not nesting—it was oozing out and there were little tiny feet inside it. Frantically, I called the vet. *"Thank you for calling. The office is closed. Office hours are 9 to 6 Monday through Friday and 9 to 12 on Saturday."* I left a message anyway and dug out the books.

him, licking, cleaning up, and eating the placenta. Fay was a mother.

Next came Battina, head first, and I performed the same procedure, clearing her lungs using the "swing" method until I heard the life-affirming squeak. She looked like a little bat and was one-third the size of Chundo.

Two more puppies arrived, one after the other, both twice as big as Battina but not as big as Chundo. The first, Crooky, had a crook in her tail and a little crooked white line on her chest. The other I named Glenn after Glenn Gould. His ears stuck out. I gave the puppies to Fay and they nursed happily, piston-like, except for Batty. She was too small. I propped her up in front of the fullest nipple and braced her feet with a brick wrapped in a towel so that she would not slide away.

I wasn't exactly ready for this occasion. Fay was a week ahead of schedule. My handyman-special whelping box was still in the basement, completed but at the moment unobtainable. Fay seemed quite happy there on the couch. What a picture! I fumbled around for my camera and took some photographs, barely bothering to focus, and guessing at the exposure setting.

Within an hour another two puppies arrived, numbers five and six, and twenty minutes later numbers seven and eight. Not until much later that evening was number nine born. He never got his strength and did not make it through the following day.

And that was it. Nine puppies: two girls, Battina and Crooky; and seven boys: Chundo, Glenn, Blaise, Ken, Speedy, Art, and Number Nine. I set up a postal scale with a little shoe box on top to weigh them and monitor their growth. Chundo was the heaviest at 12 oz., and Battina was the lightest at 4 oz. All the rest were between 7 and 9 oz. I noticed in the photographs that Battina was always next to Chundo. They were together in the birth canal, too, and to this day are still close. I wonder if any of the others buddied up. I didn't think to look for it at the time.

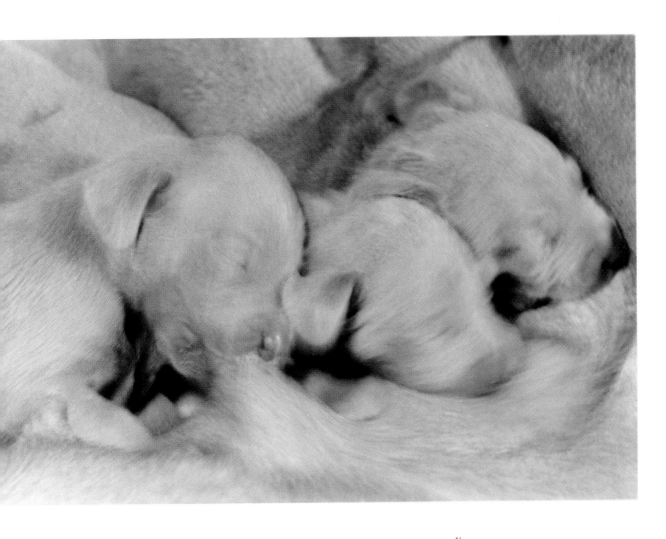

Nursery

Sleep

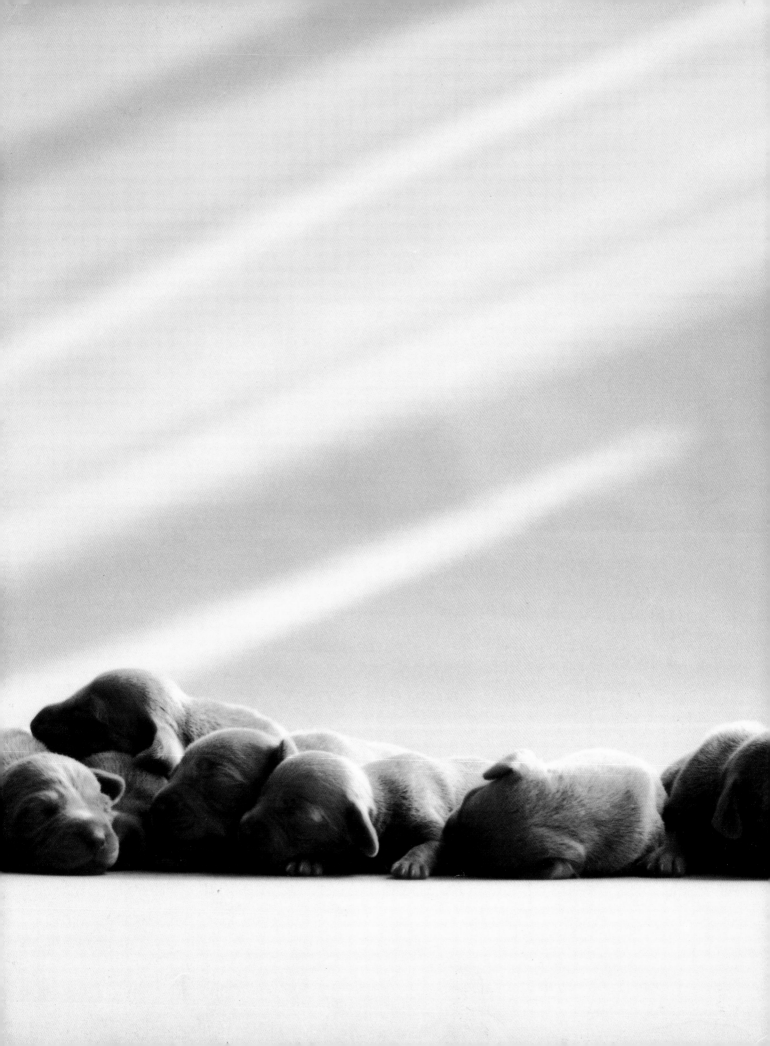

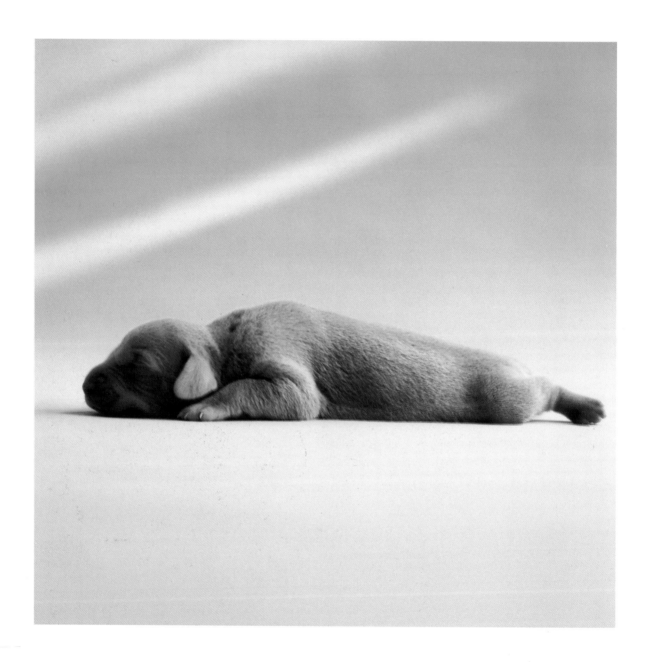

Slope

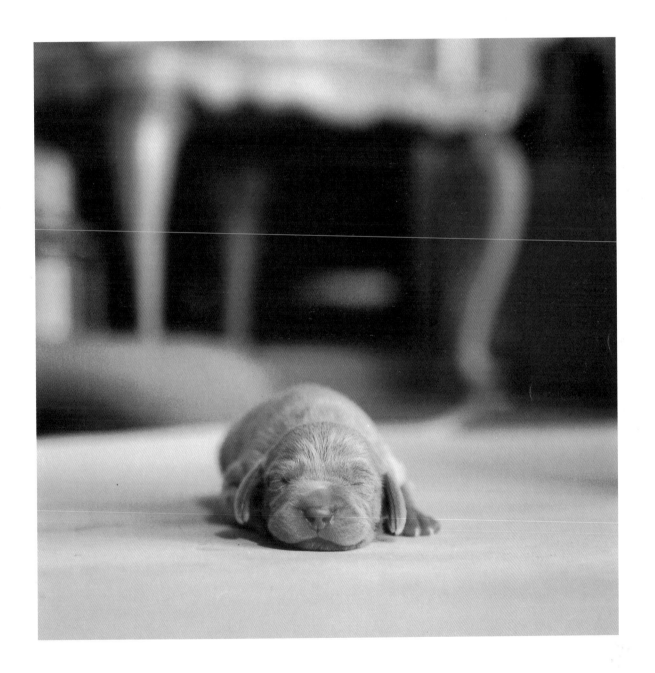

Little Big Head

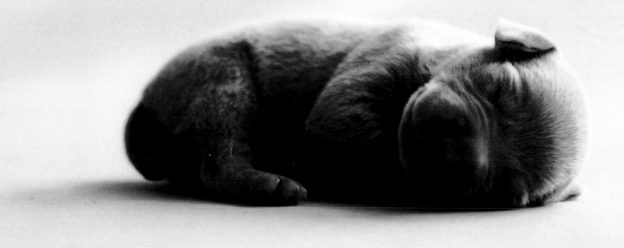

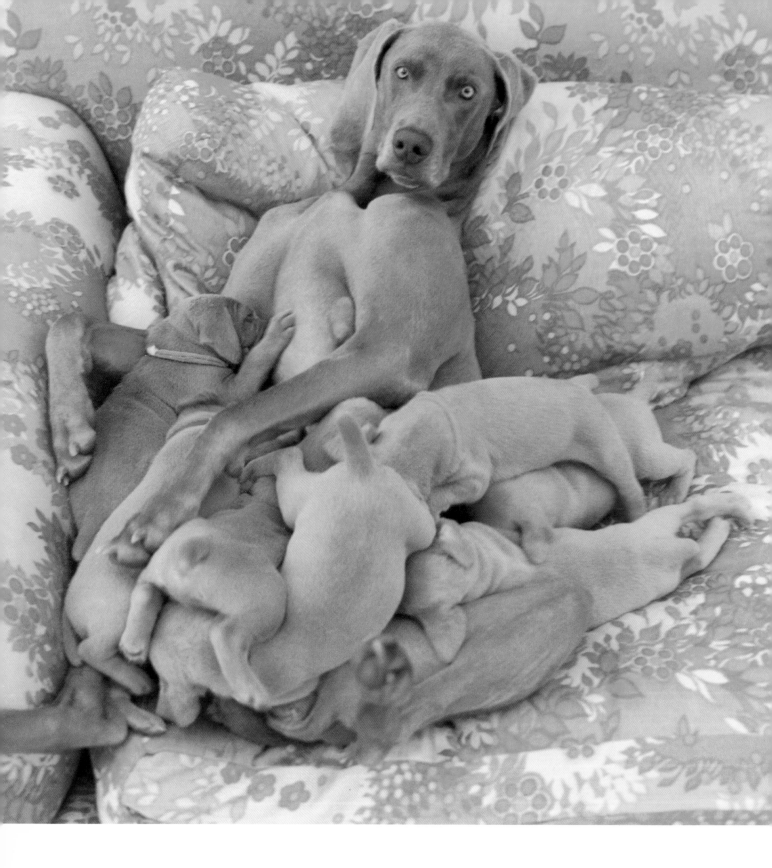

Mother's Day

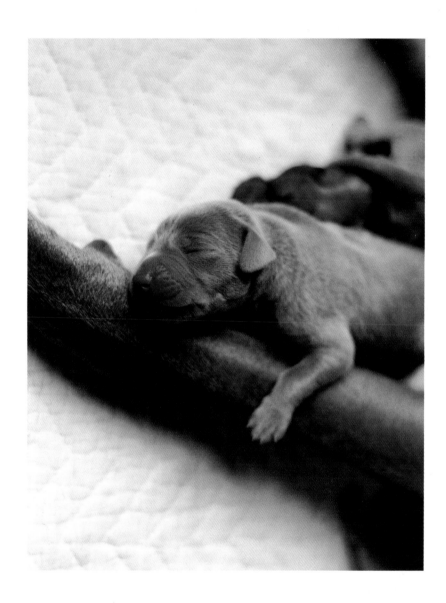

Arm and Leg

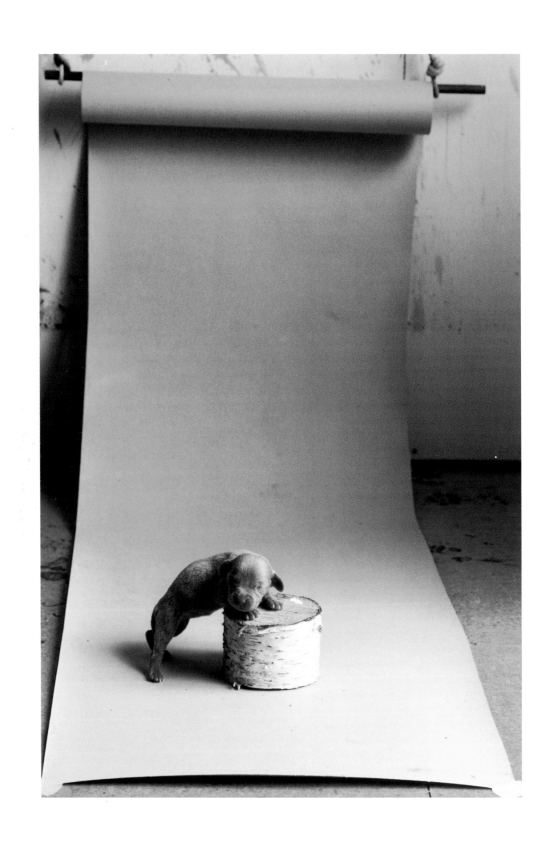

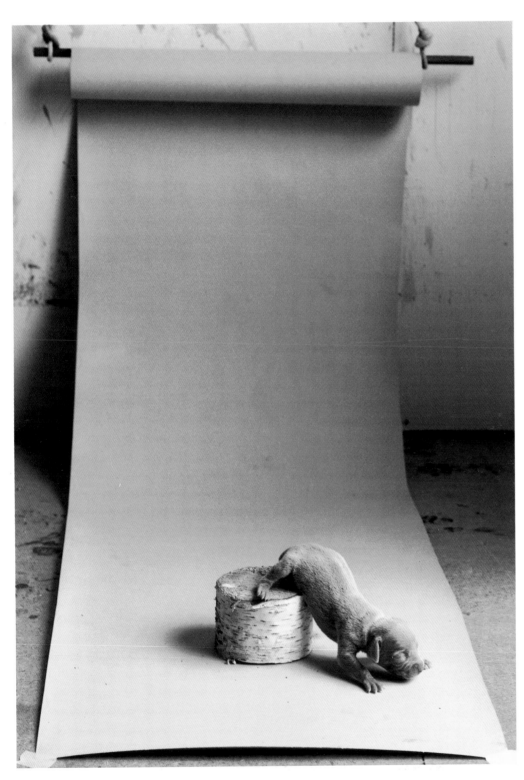

Early Work

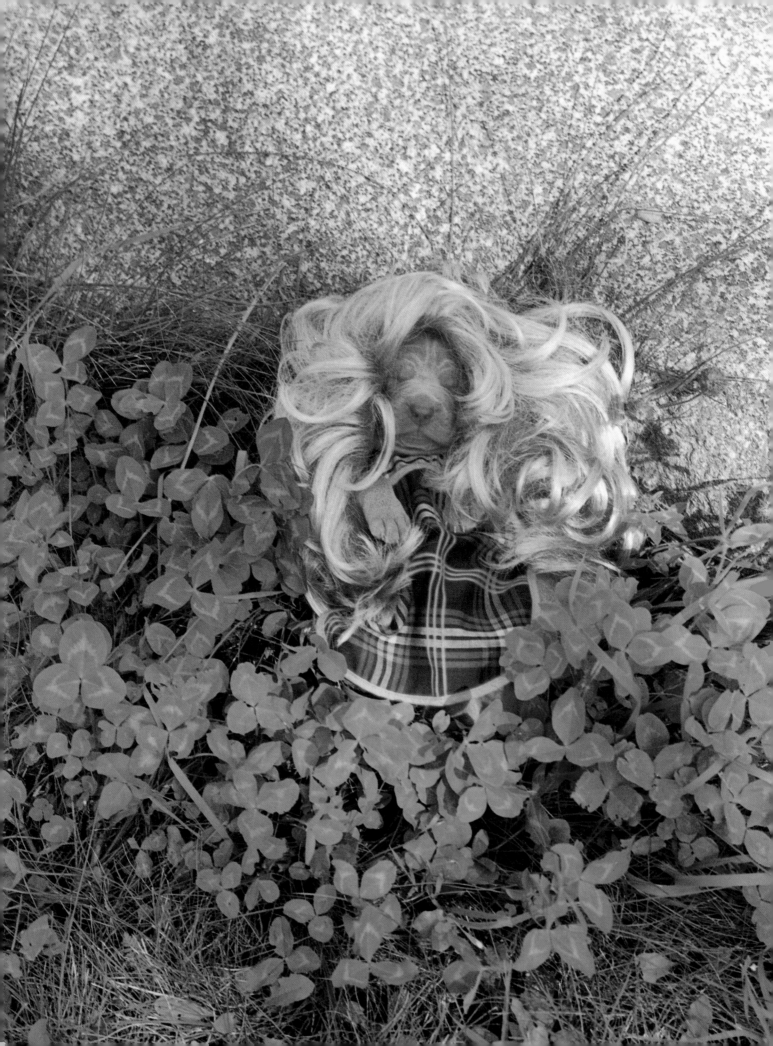

More alien than

cute.

Photographing puppies in the first two weeks is simple. Just set them down, or up, and shoot. Group them together in various formations. Watch them flow into one another—one organism, seeking heat and its mother's scent. Their eyes don't open until they are about two weeks old.

Fay didn't mind me photographing her and her puppies. She looked sweet and slightly cross-eyed, high on life. *"Fay, can I borrow Crooky and Blaise for a minute?"* She did, however, pay close attention whenever I took a puppy away for a picture. As long as they were in view, Fay was okay. But separating one from the rest was upsetting to the puppies. They needed to be returned quickly to their mates. Chundo and Batty didn't seem to mind as much, so I usually picked on them. Right from the beginning they were the most outstanding, although I took turns having favorites.

I had never worked with puppies this young. Man Ray was six weeks old when I got him. Fay was really a young adult when I began working with her at one year. Most puppies you see in pictures are two or three months old. That is the age when they are at their maximum cuteness, the cuddly-bear greeting card phase.

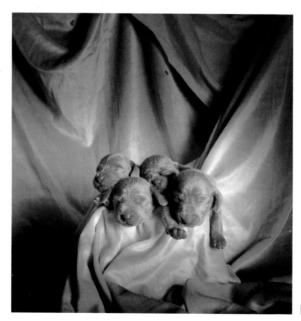

Nature Morte

Previous page: Rock and Clover

I loaded them into a cardboard box and ventured out into a green field.

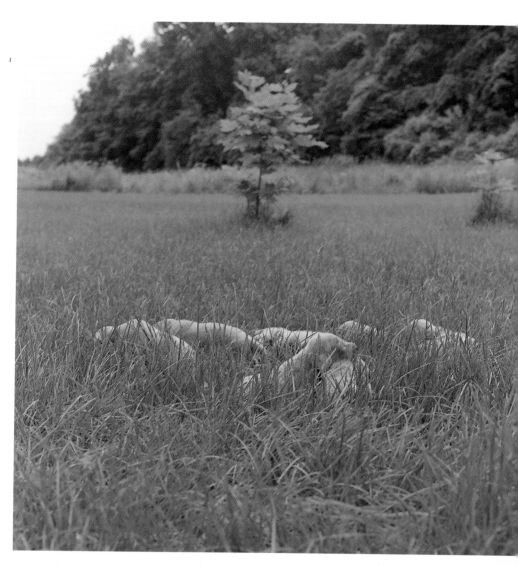

We all know the look—irresistible but familiar just the same.

At a couple of days old, the puppies were more alien than cute. Their tiny foot pads and flip-tab ears made them look like cheaply made vinyl toys. Their ears were sealed shut, as were their soft, bulging eye sockets. And they were striped! These markings were to fade to gray in three days, which is typical, but at that moment, when I first began to photograph them, the puppies were the most beautiful velvety gray with silver stripes running down their backs.

When the puppies were one week old, I loaded them into a cardboard box and ventured out into a green field.

Fay followed closely. I put them in a pile at the edge of the woods, took a meter reading, and photographed them from various angles. They looked like moles. When I brought them back inside, I counted seven puppies. I made a personal best fifty-yard dash back to the location. No puppy. My heart was pounding. I was about to return for a recount when I heard a peep coming from the woods....

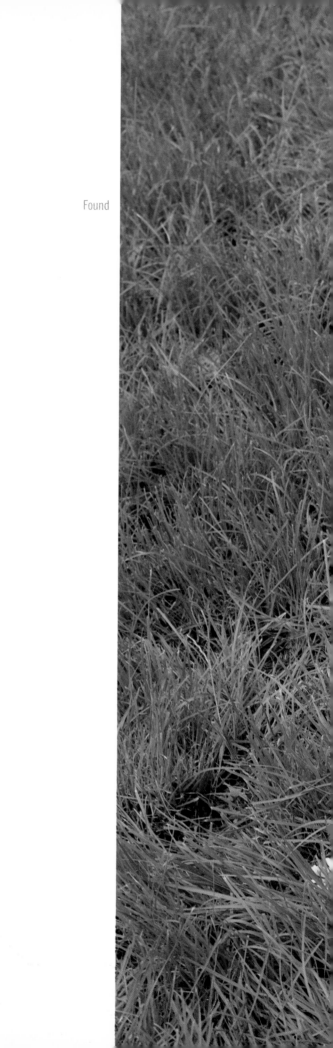

Found

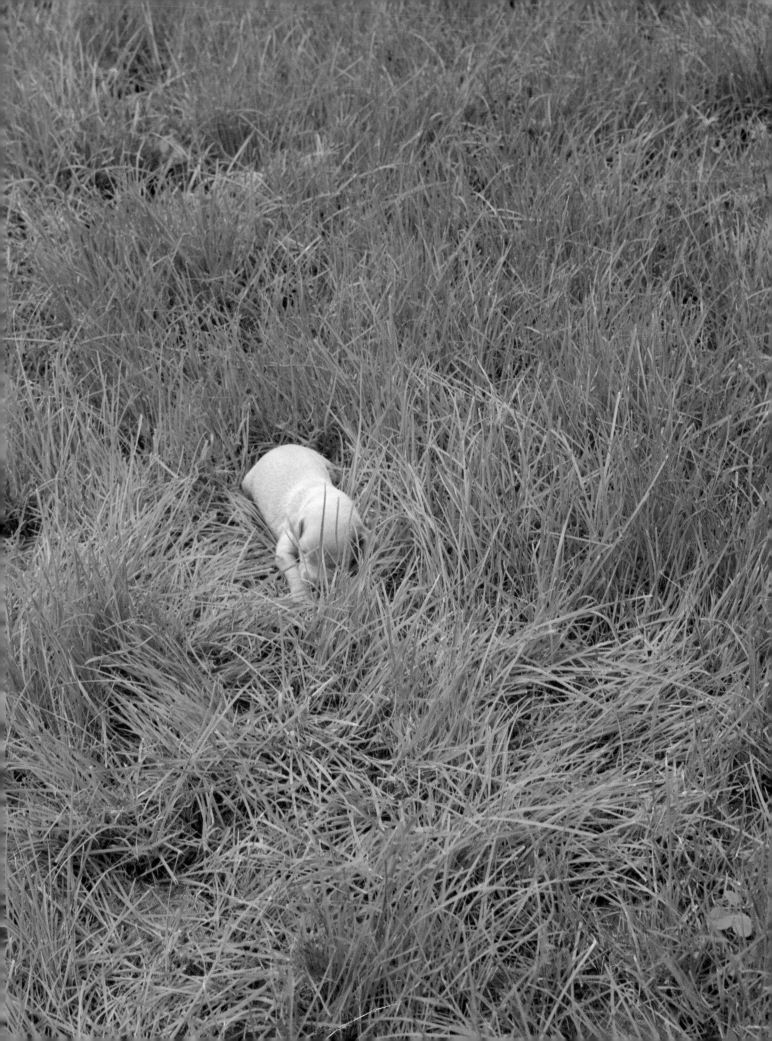

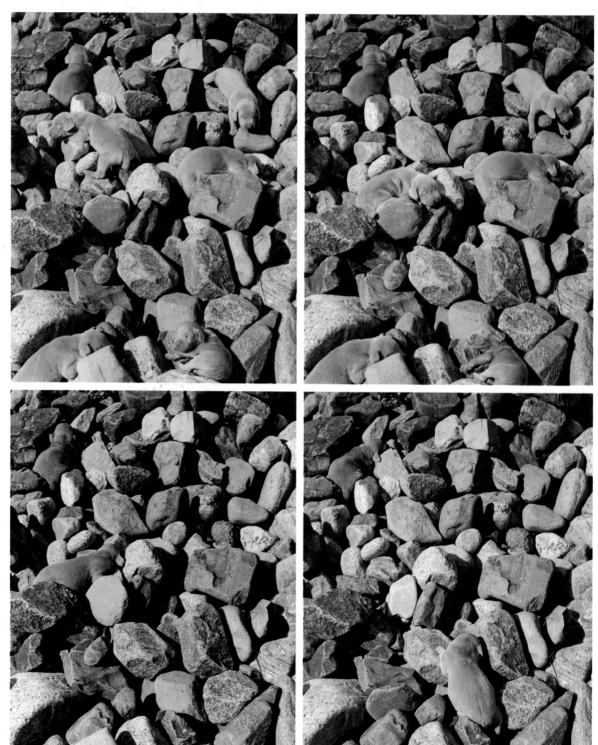

Rocks and Stones

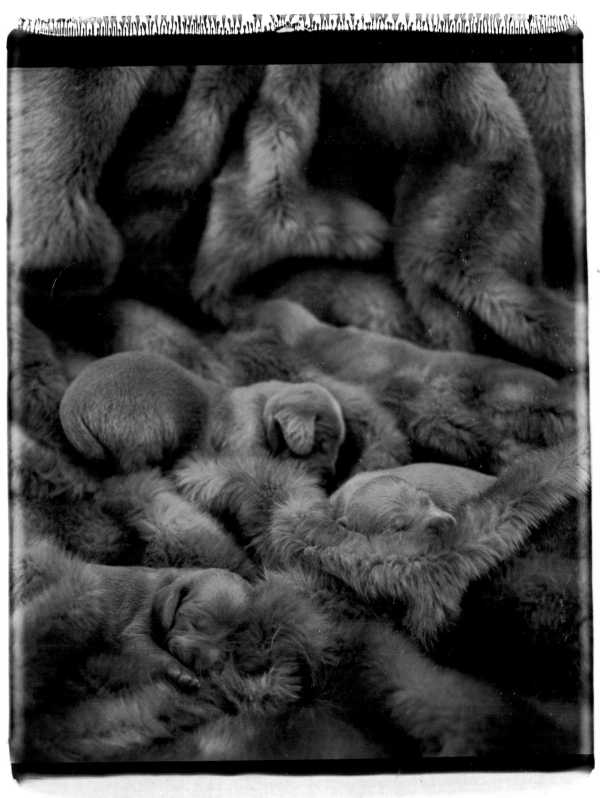

Burrow

Cottage

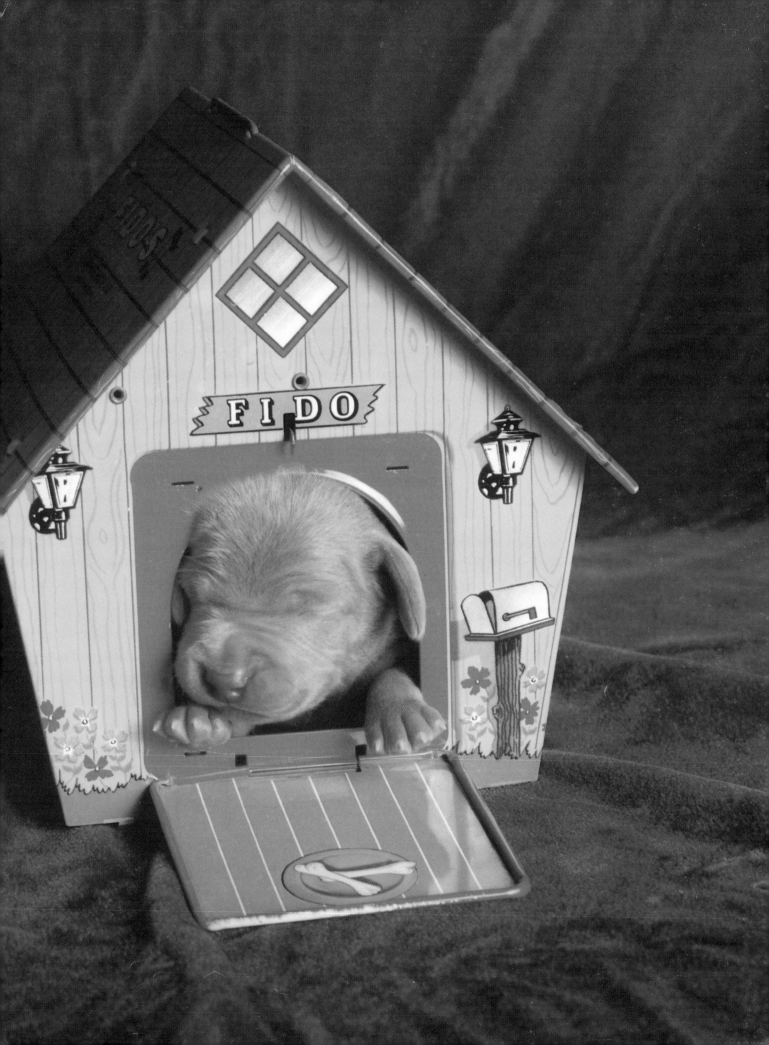

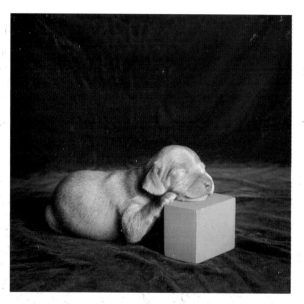

Orange Block

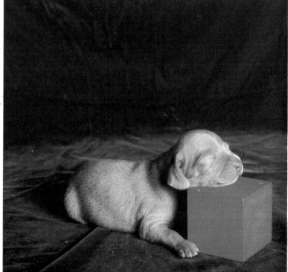

Red Cube

Block Bridge

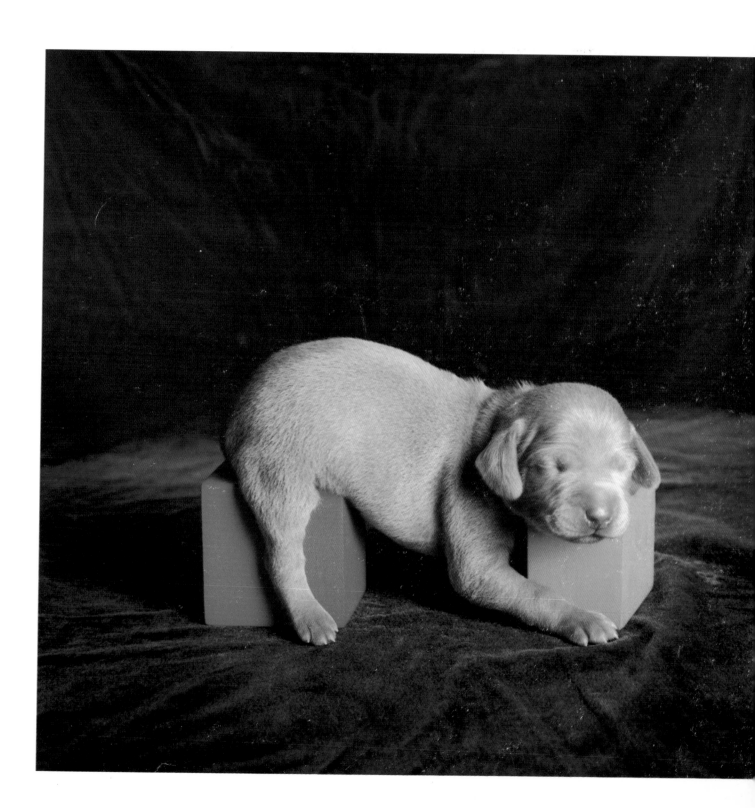

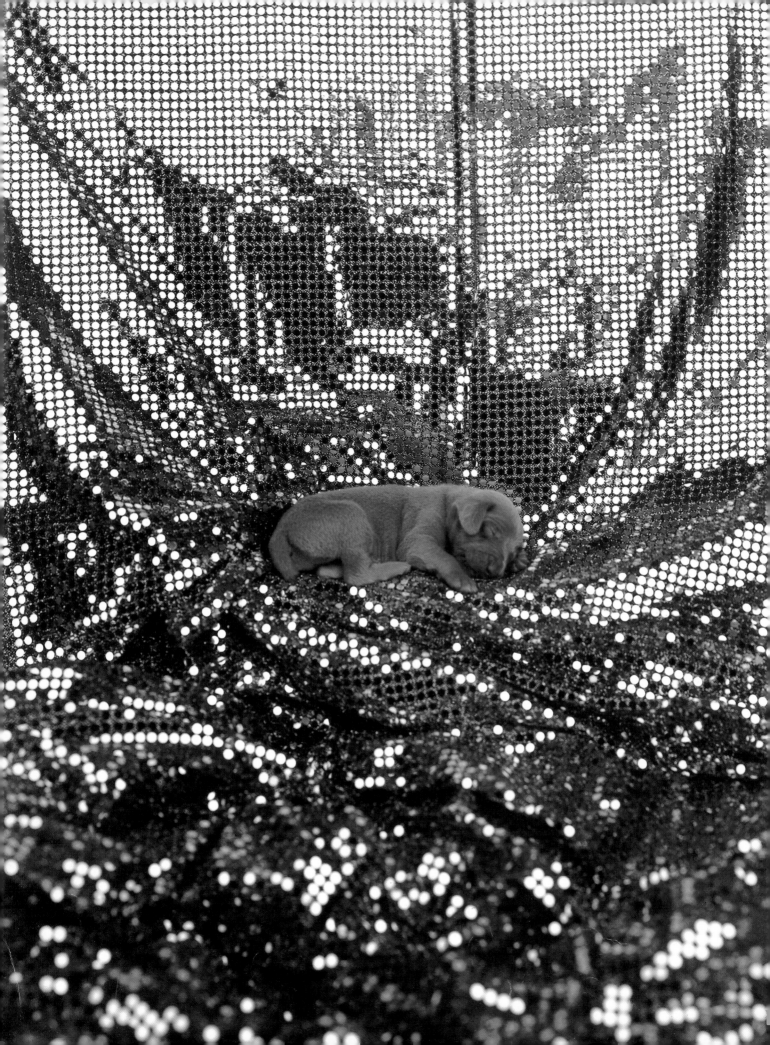

Sled Dog

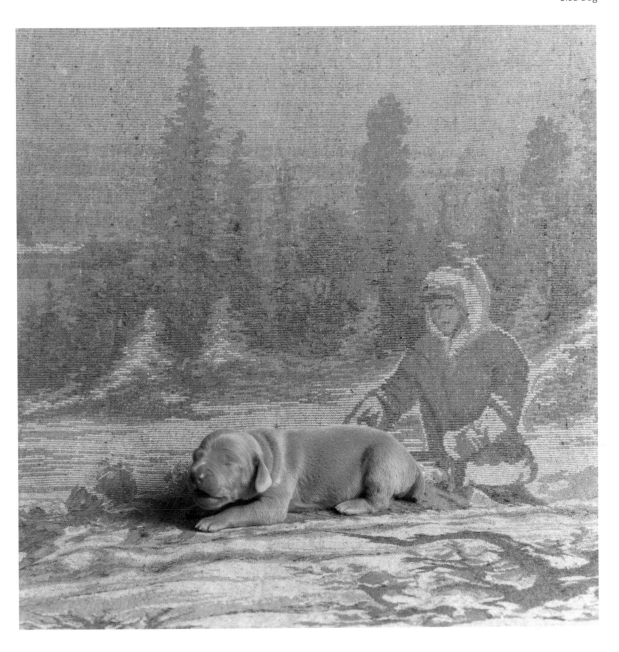

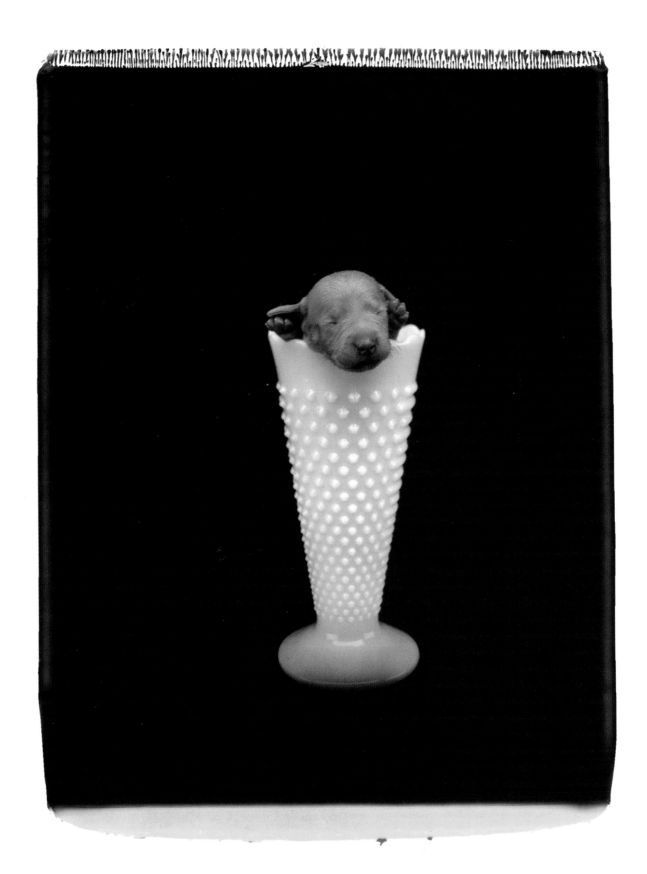

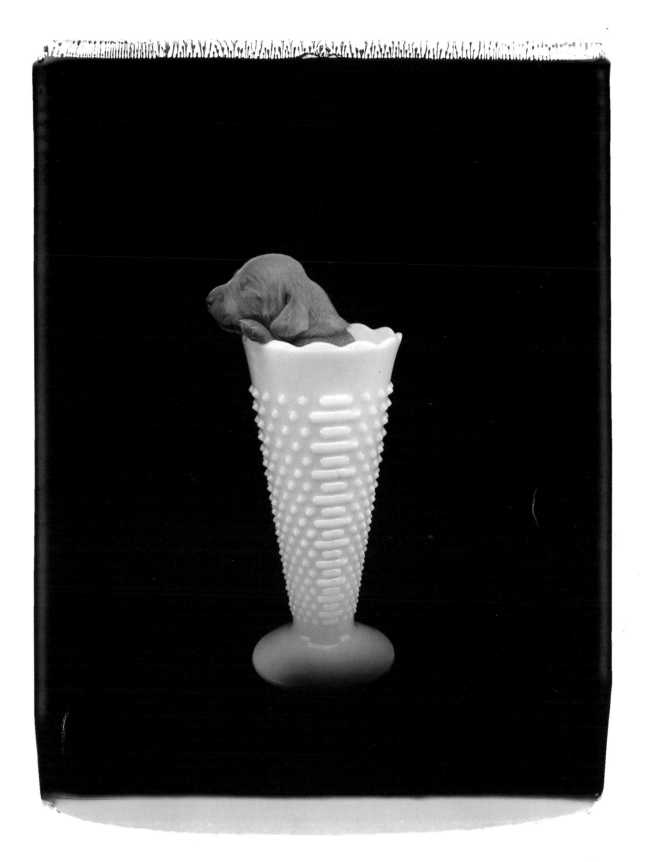

Vase

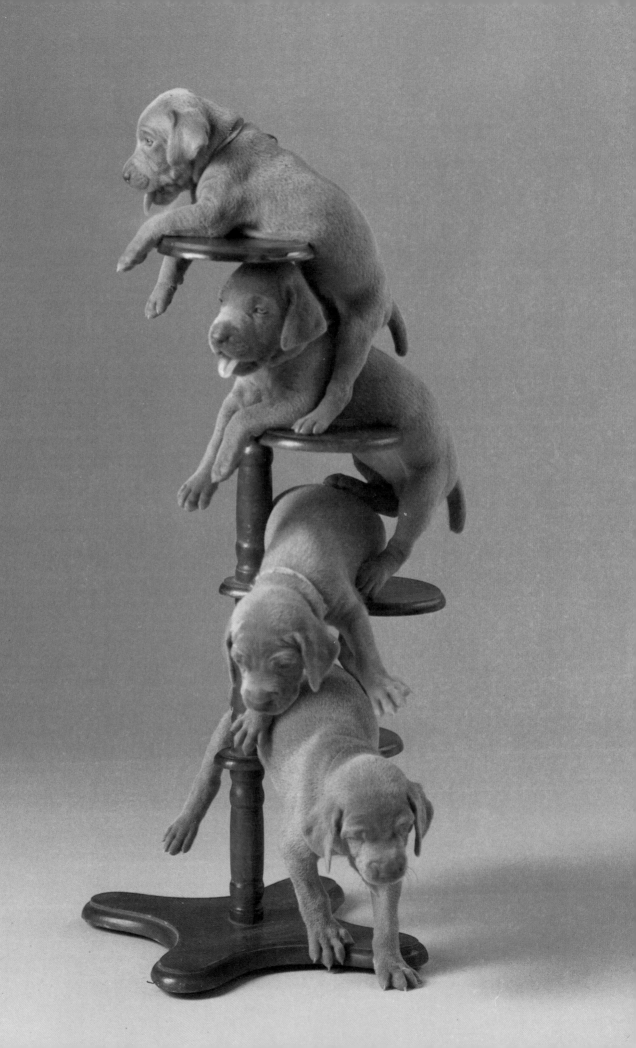

Puppy Planter

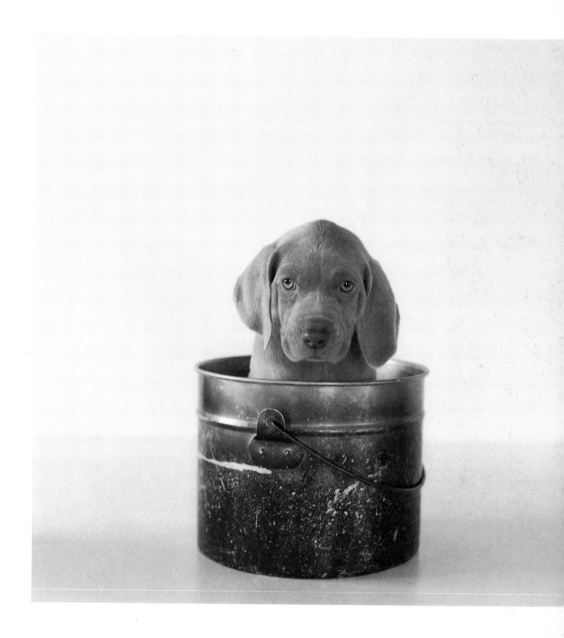

Pup Pot

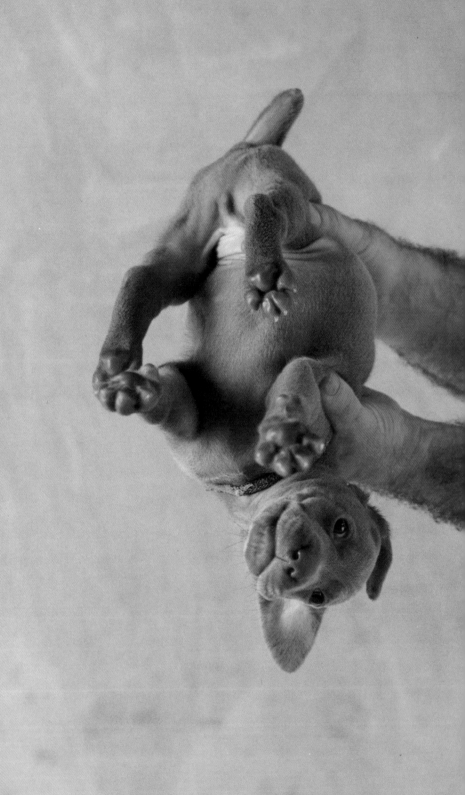

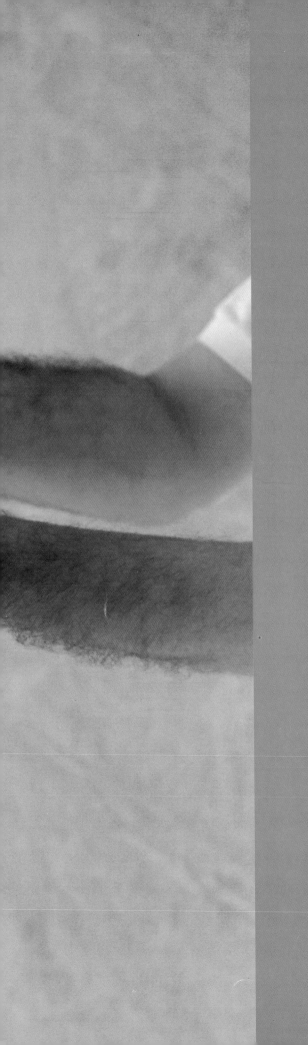

Joy, surprise,

lightness.

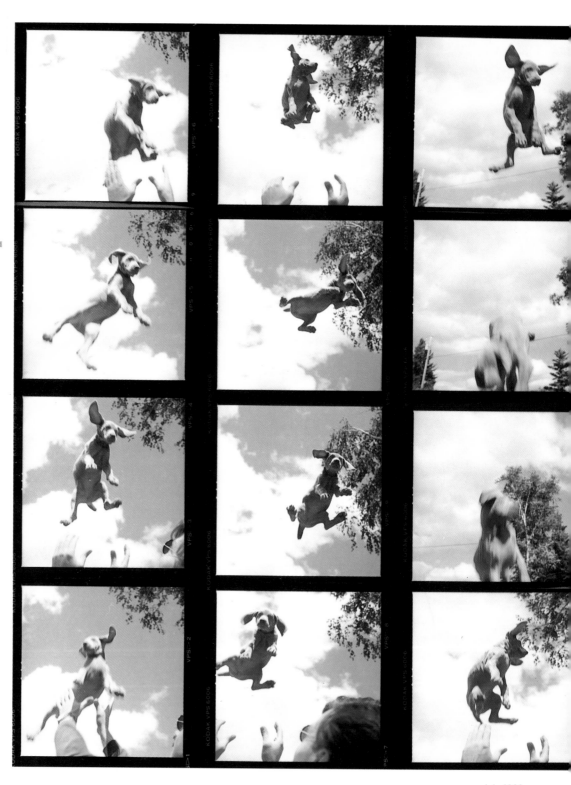

July 1989

Previous page: Upside-Down

These days were
breathtaking,
the most eventful
since their birth,
and the pictures
from this second
week of their lives
are among the
most memorable.

On day thirteen, the puppies' eyes began to open: a brilliant blue light beaming through. In a few days, all eyes were open. Chundo's were the bluest and remained blue even as those of the others faded to the amber-yellow typical of weimaraners. I could now see *into* the puppies. They were real beings.

I moved Fay and her puppies to the screened-in back porch, which was bathed in a light that was particularly beautiful and soft that day, and I hung one of my unfinished paintings as a neutral backdrop. My assistant Kathleen snapped the shutter on my camera while I tossed and caught each puppy, one at a time. Joy, surprise, lightness, peace— almost every frame reveals another mood, a different physical state. One creature looks like a rocket launched, another one is coming in for a landing. One appears cocooned in orbit, another hovers in space, suspended just at the crest. In some pictures, my outstretched hands are caught in the frame, along with the subject. At this age they behave more like rag dolls than dogs. In their trust in us, they are oblivious.

Flying Puppy

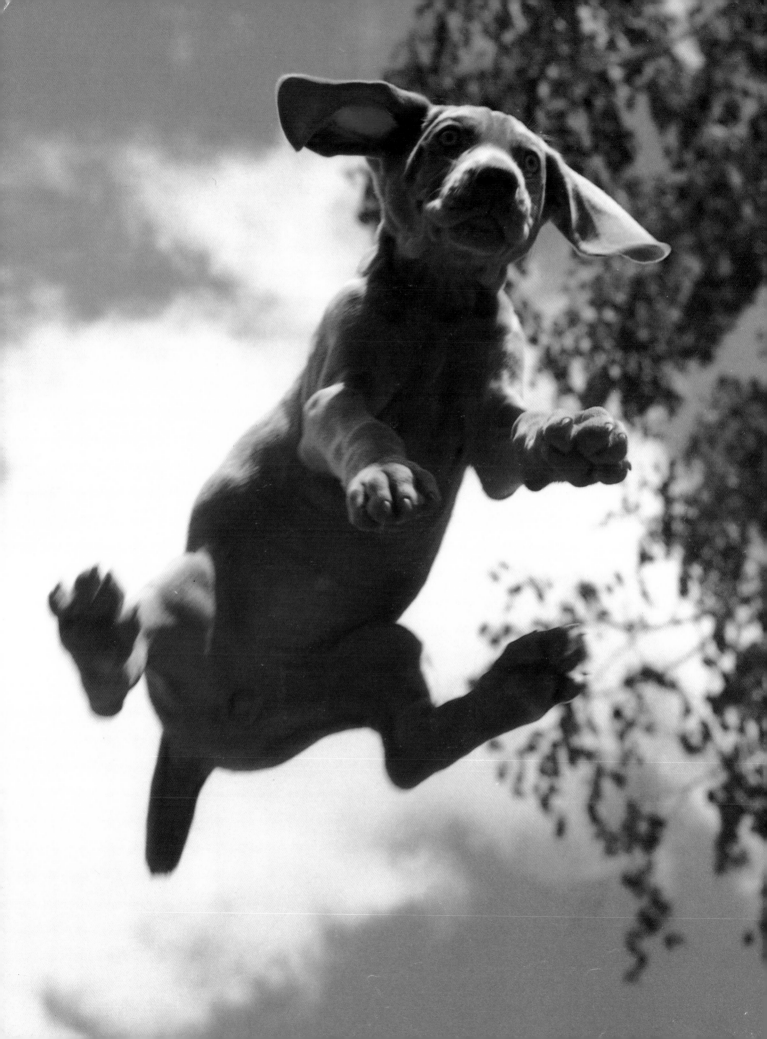

Trampoline

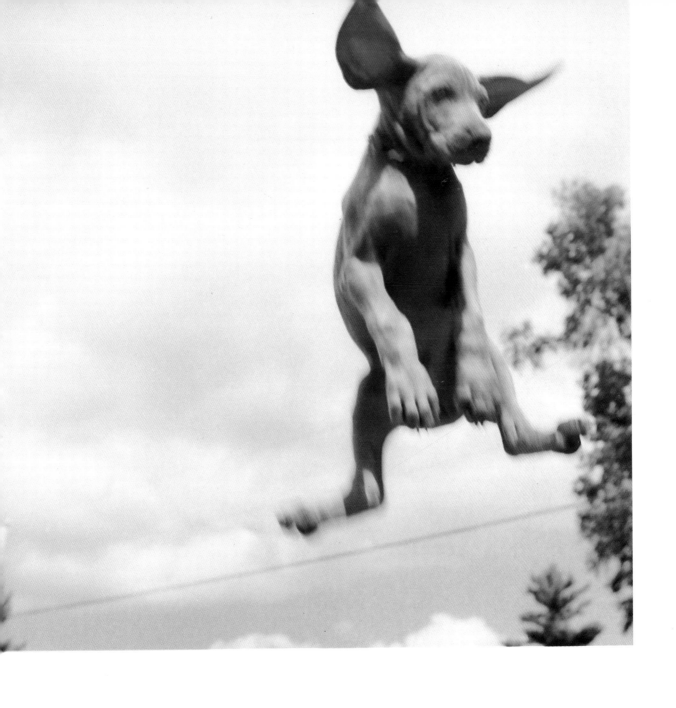

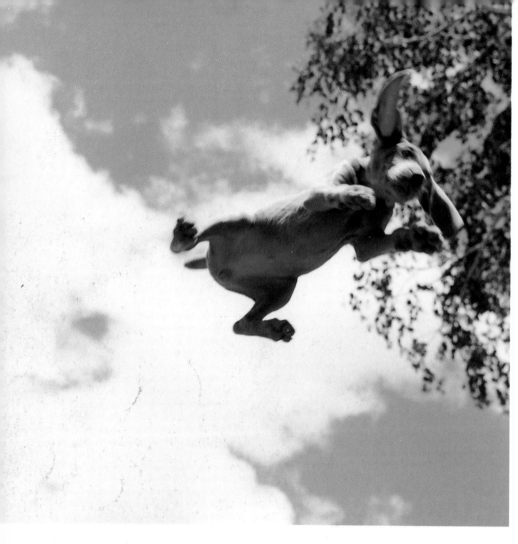

Cannonball

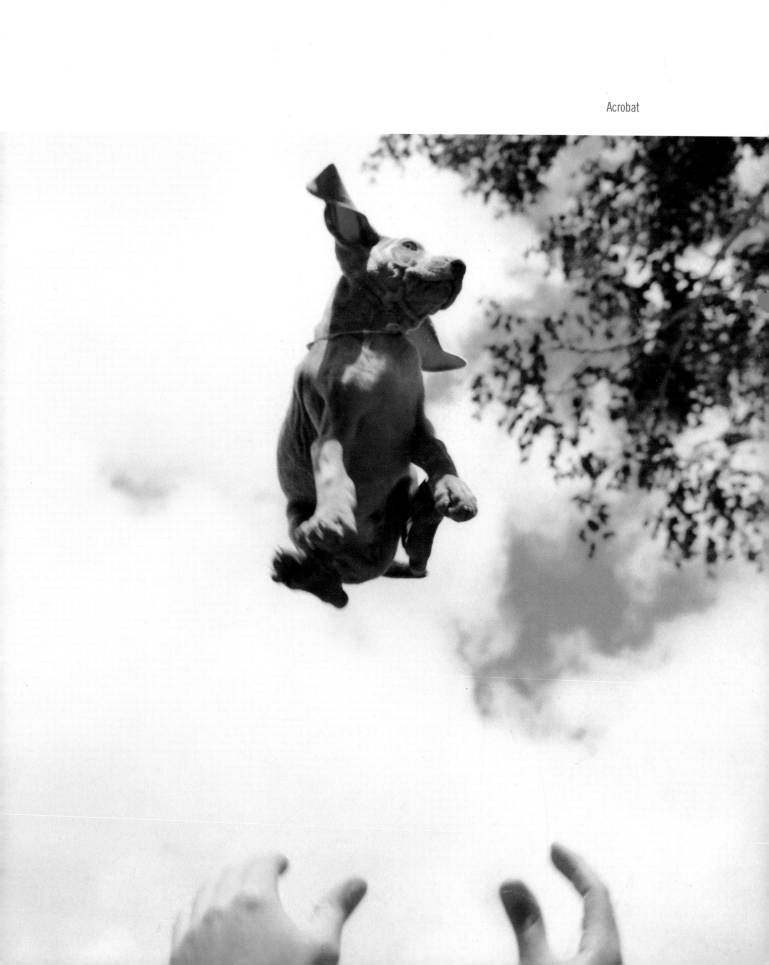

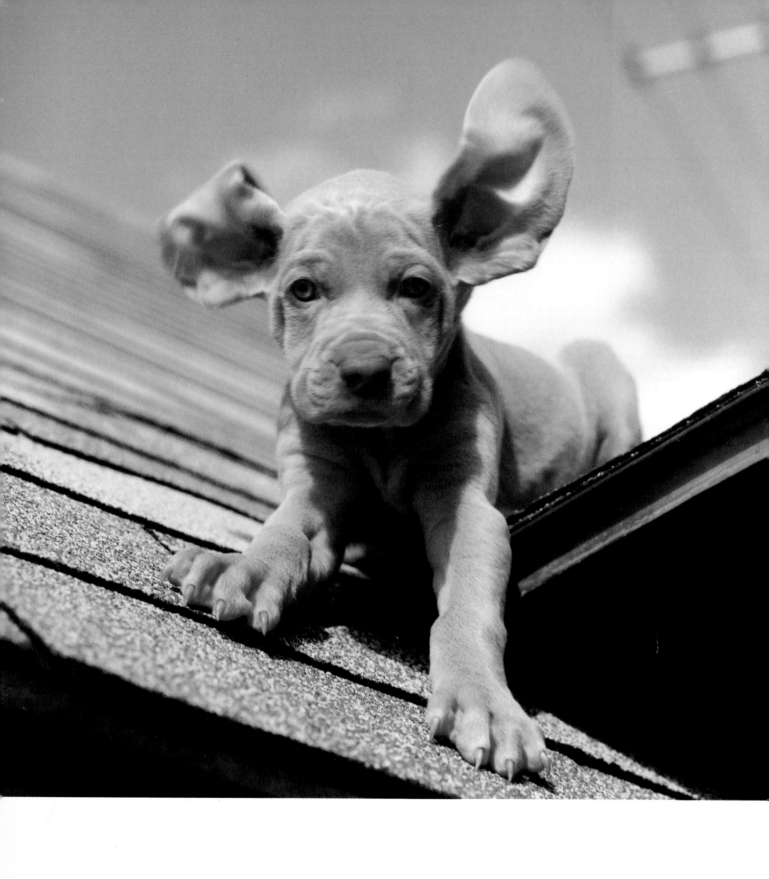

Landing

Flying Dumbo

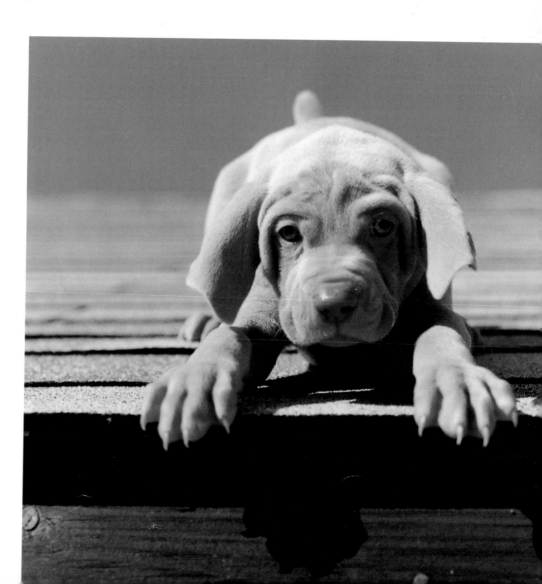

Hand Held

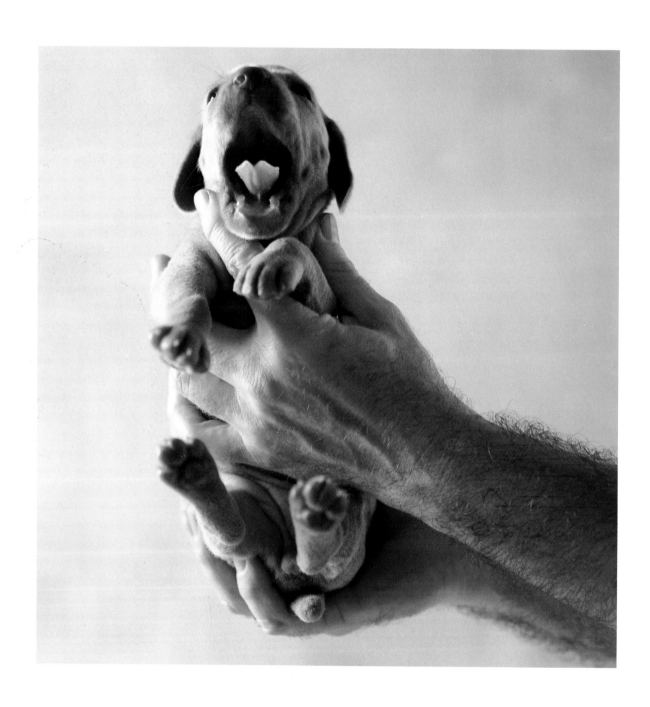

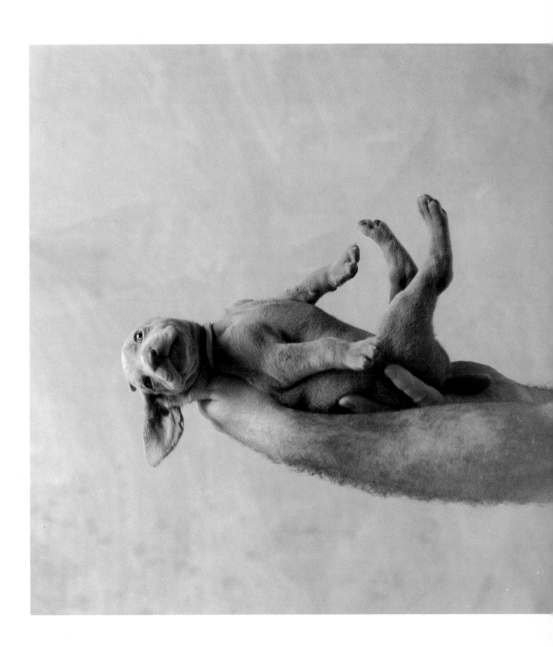

Cradle

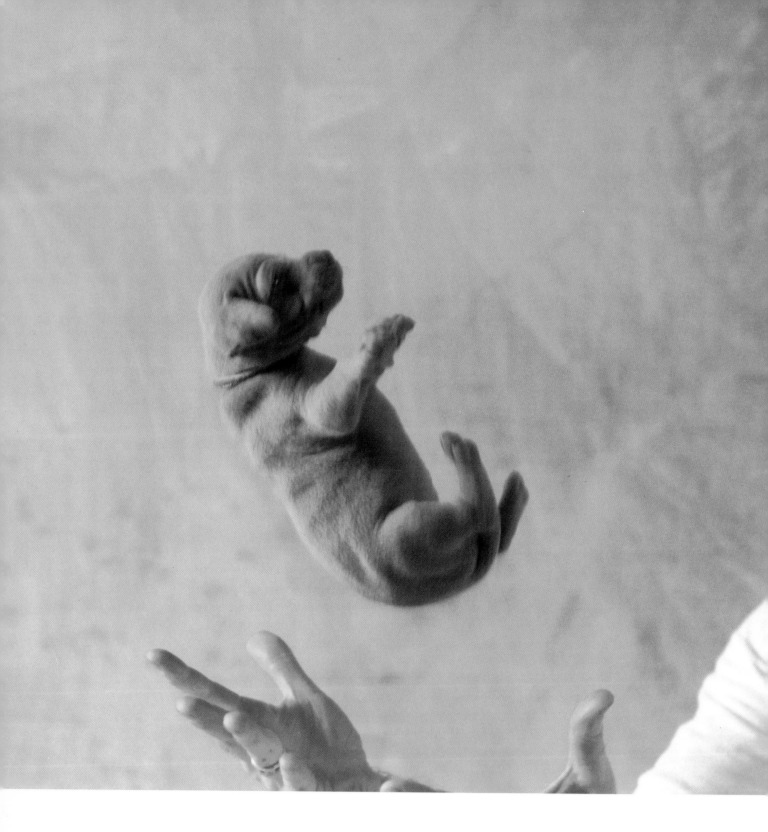

Orbit

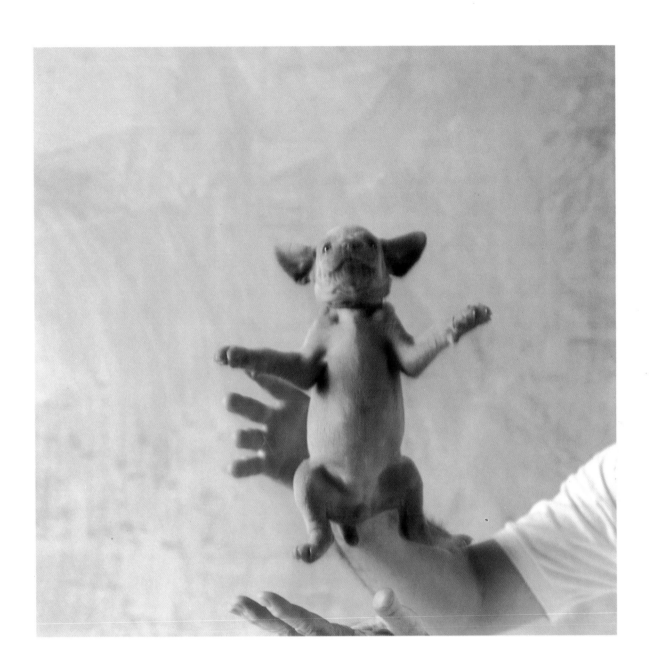

Launch

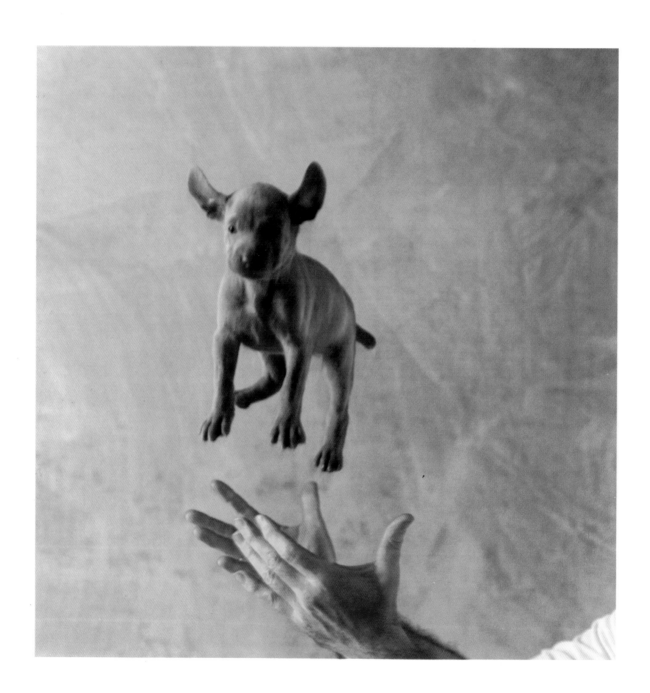

Airborne

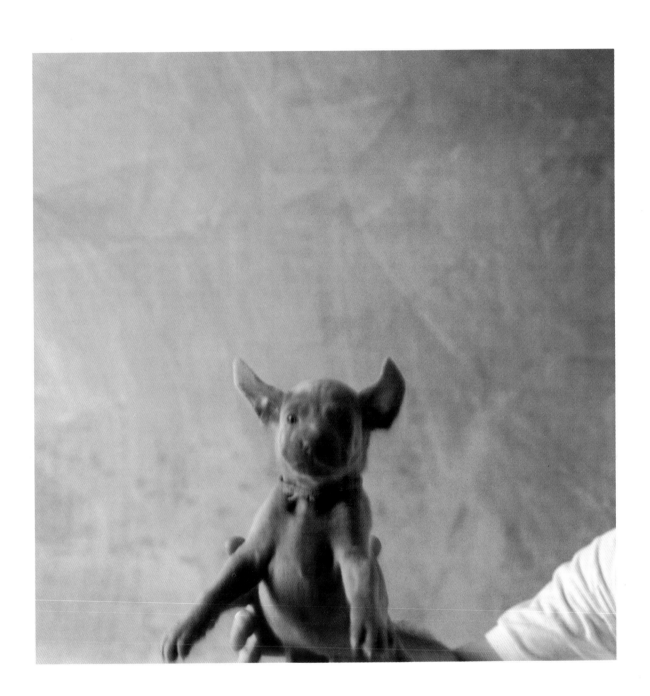

Return

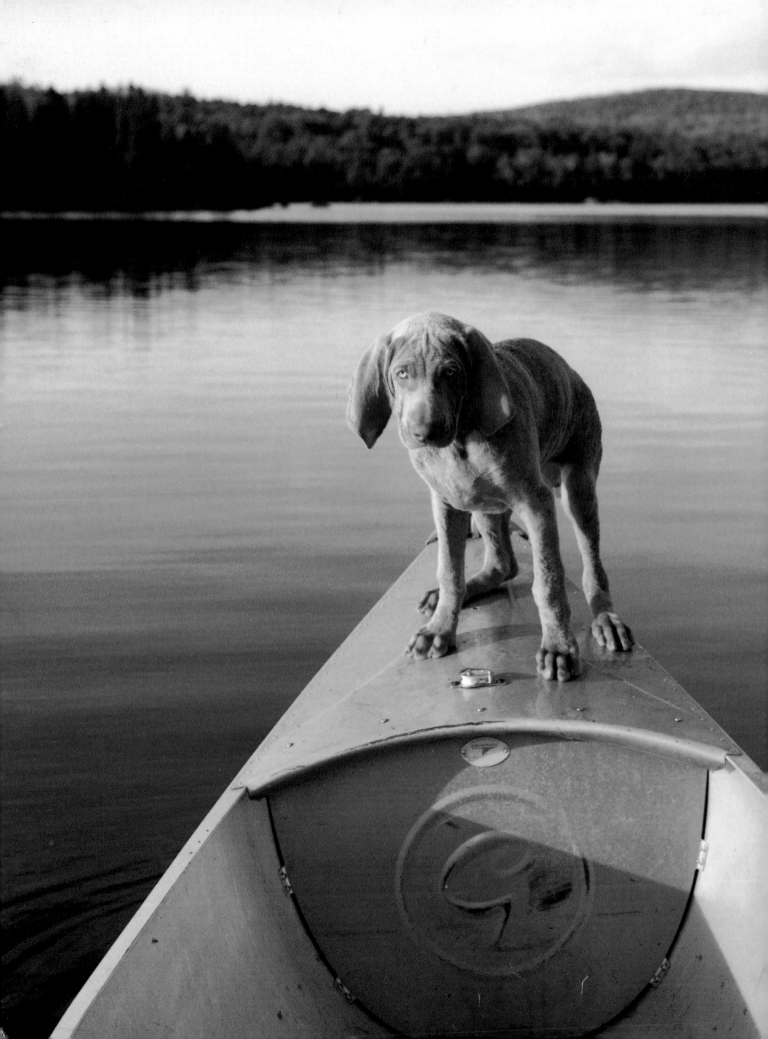

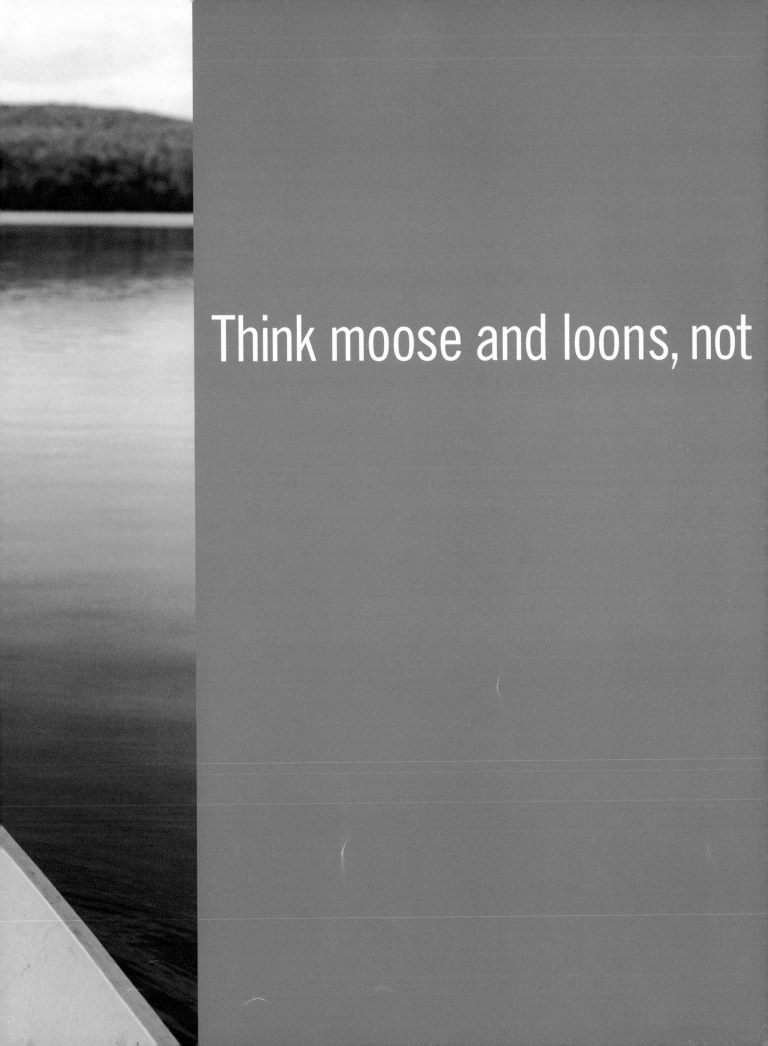

Think moose and loons, not

lobsters.

On the first of July, when the puppies were twenty days old, I packed everyone in the Jeep and moved from upstate New York to my cabin in Maine (think moose and loons not lobsters and Bushes).

I had first come to the Rangeley Lakes region in the fall of 1977 and had returned every summer since. I had just acquired the lodge adjacent to my cabin, a large rambling structure built a hundred years ago. Not designed for living, the lodge had been the main building of the Hardly Inn— *"Rustic Modernization in the Heart of the Woods"*—and had received guests and housed dining, laundry, and game rooms until it closed in 1961. In the summer of 1989, the lodge became a weimaraner habitat. I can still hear the puppies thundering down the long fenced-in porch to greet me in the morning.

After four weeks, the puppies were weaned and Fay no longer wanted any part of them. She jumped in and out of their pen for the briefest of moments. Photographing the rambunctious puppies became more of a challenge. You couldn't just put them down anywhere and expect them to be there by the time you read the meter and set up the camera. You had to carefully select the puppy and the place. Posing became easier if I gave the puppies something specific to

Previous page: Voyager

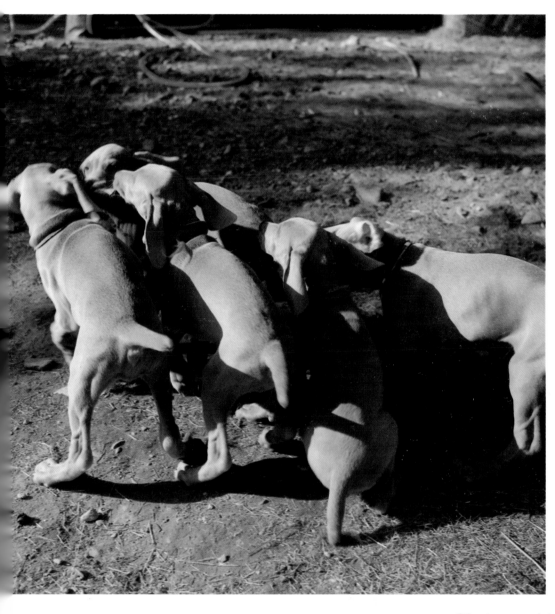

Rugby

Photographing
the rambunctious
puppies became
more of a challenge.

Marigolds, Petunias, Weimaraners
(Left to Right: Chundo, Battina, Glenn, Blaise, Ken, Speedy, Crooky, and Art)

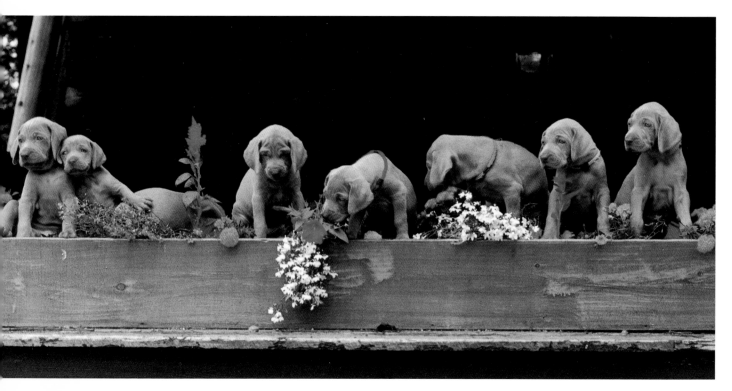

do—form a bridge, stand on a rock, sit on a dock, stay in a wheelbarrow—but still I needed help. I taught Adam, a six-year-old neighbor, to read the light meter and be my photo assistant for the summer. Once, Adam was in charge of Crooky, whom I was photographing atop a stack of hay bales. *"Make sure she doesn't fall, Adam.... Adam?!"* I heard an *oomph*. Crooky was no longer atop the hay bales. *"11.8, Bill. No make that 8.11,"* Adam continued reading. Crooky escaped injury, but I became more cautious and enlisted more help. Not surprisingly, this was not difficult. Everyone on the lake came by often to see the puppies. They all wanted to hold them. *"My turn." "No, my turn." "You already had a turn."*

I read that six weeks was an ideal time to introduce the puppies to water. Although not pure water dogs like Labs or Chesapeakes, who go out of their way to walk through a mud puddle, weimaraners are good swimmers. I carted the litter down to the dock, assigned two friends to lifeguard duty, and slid the puppies one at a time into the lake. Only Batty failed to pass the water test, flailing so intensely that she flipped herself over. She had the buoyancy of an old metal wind-up toy. I had to fish her out with my boat net. But Batty began to distinguish herself in other ways.

When playing, Batty acted more like a kitten than a puppy in her ability to entertain herself. One game, "complicated ball" I called it, was played with a tennis ball and the rungs of a straight-backed chair. The game resembled pinball, and when playing she didn't seem to need me or her mates. Fay liked Batty, but there were times when she became jealous of the attention Batty's games received. After one particularly joyous episode of "complicated ball," Fay became so incensed that she blasted Batty with a tremendously angry bark. This devastated Batty. So much for "complicated ball." After that the mere sight of a tennis ball made her ill.

I was mad at Fay for killing the game and taking away the sport, but I think she was fed up with all the noise. The pack thing was getting to be too much. At eight weeks it was time to thin the herd. By the end of the summer we found homes for five of the puppies. Of the remaining three, Chundo and Crooky would stay in Maine (where we are reunited every summer)—Chundo to live with my sister Pam, and Crooky with Dave McMillan, a friend and the Rangeley town dentist. Batty would go back to New York with me and Fay.

I have never doubted my choice in dogs.

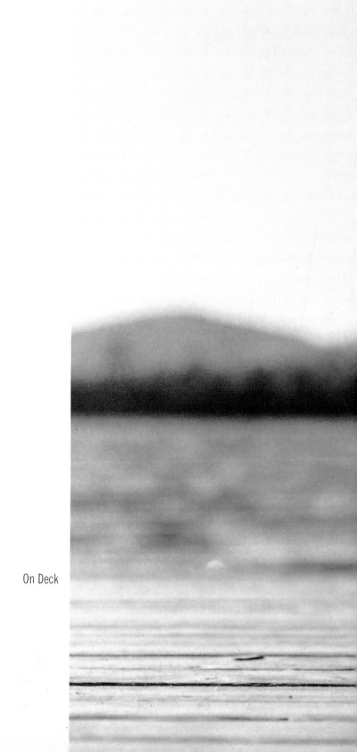

On Deck

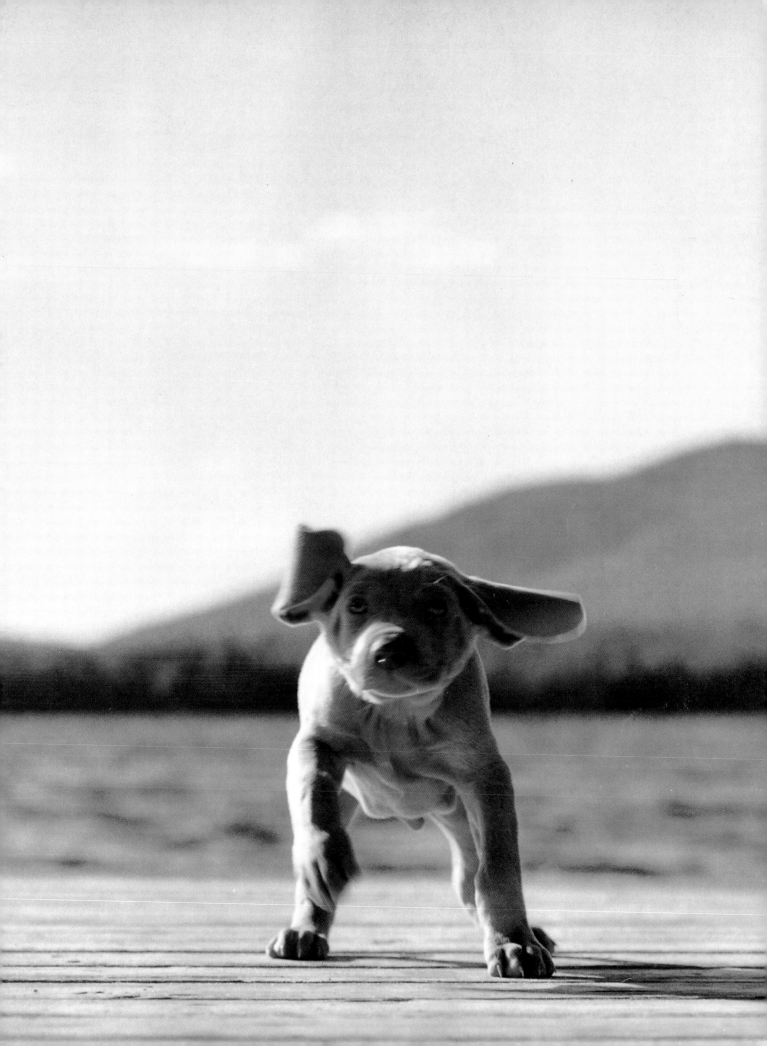

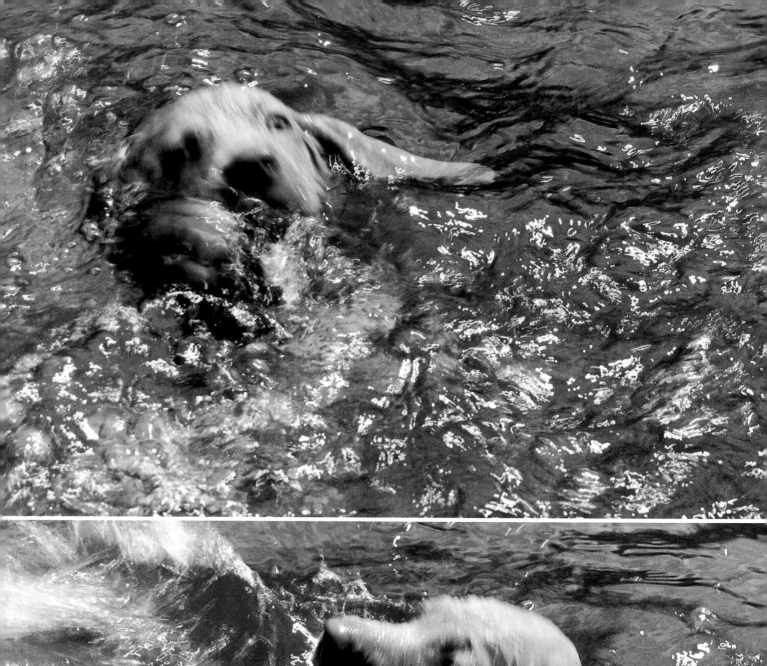
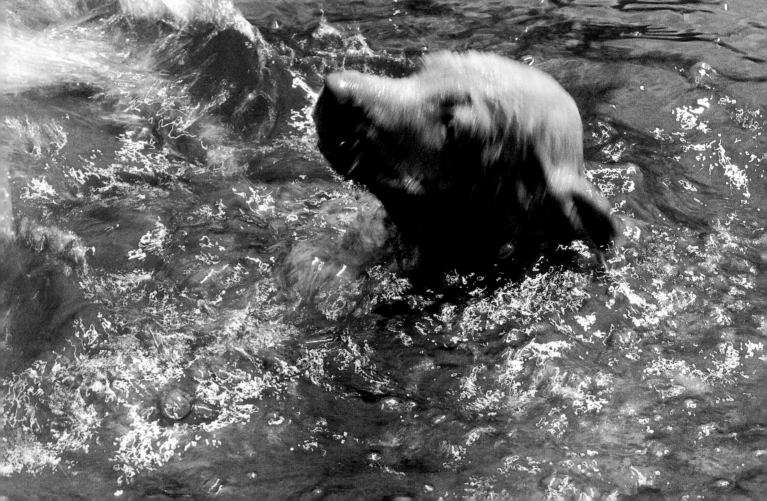

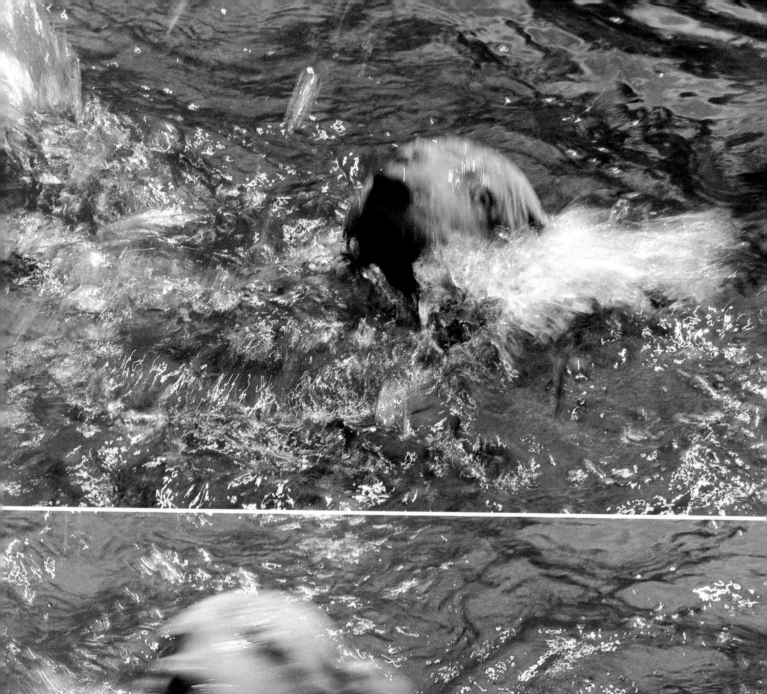
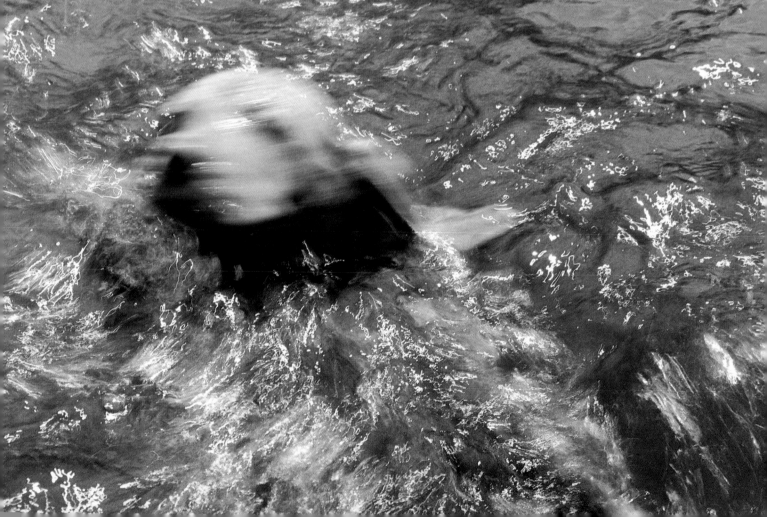

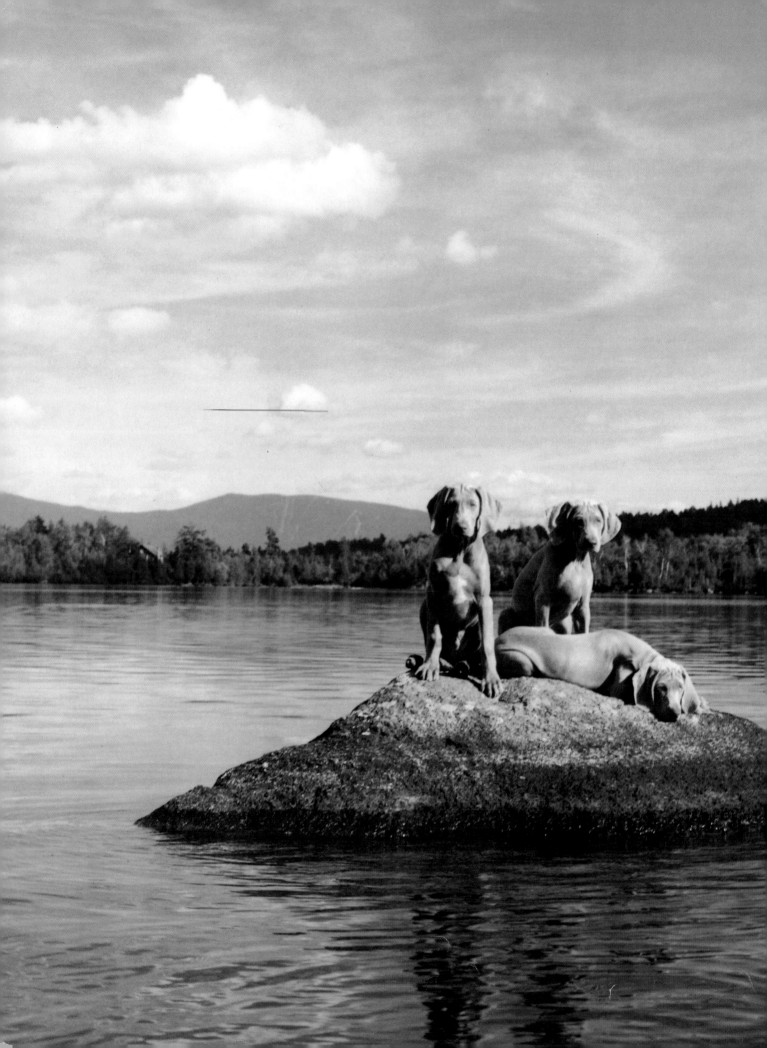

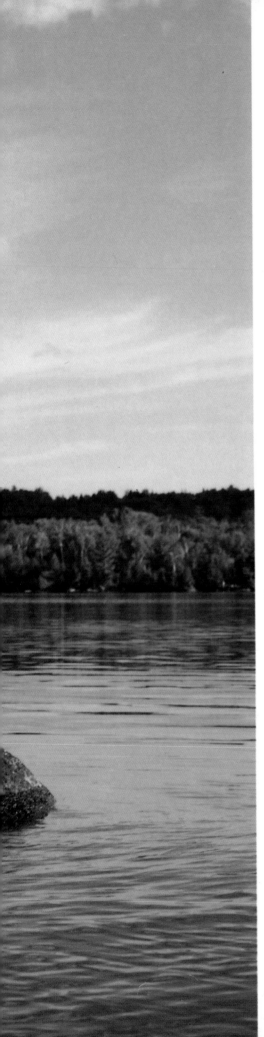

Puppy Island

Previous page: Swim

Lakeside

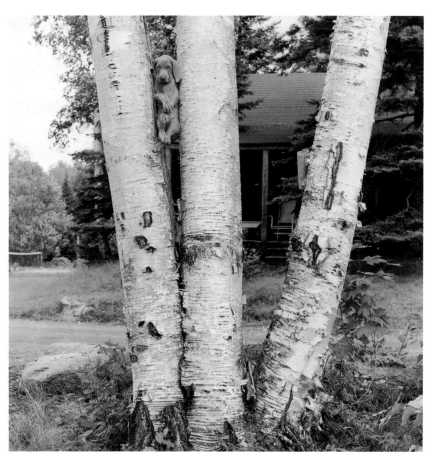

Birdhouse

Wedgeman

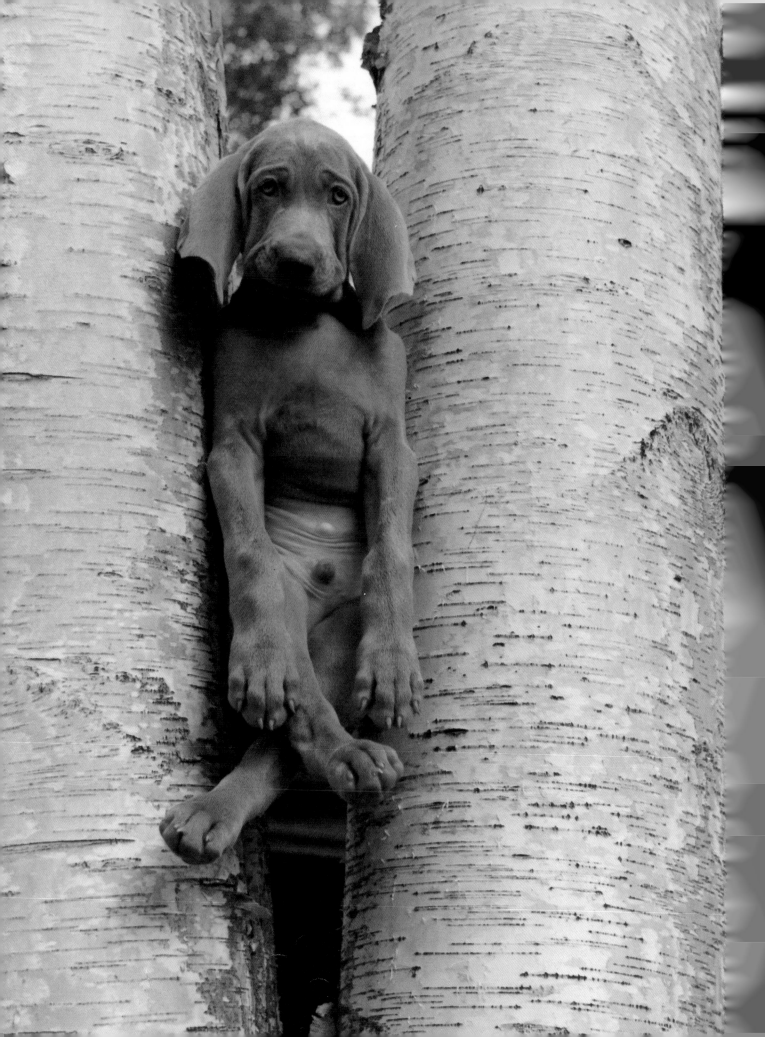

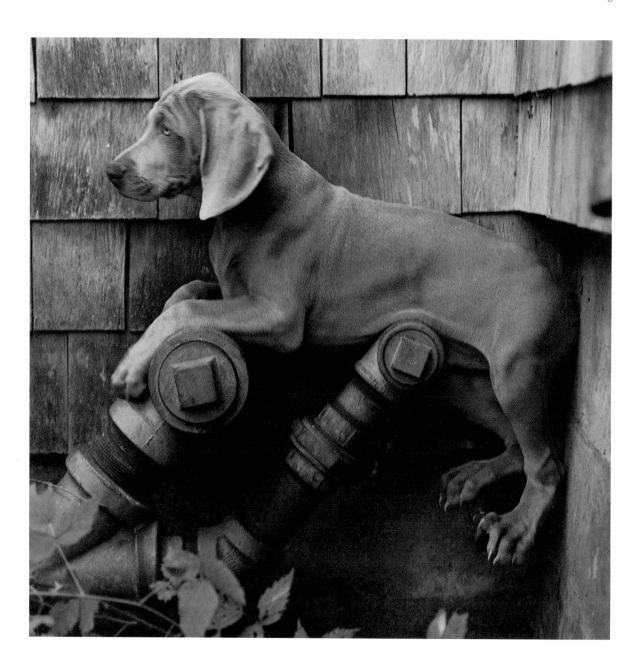

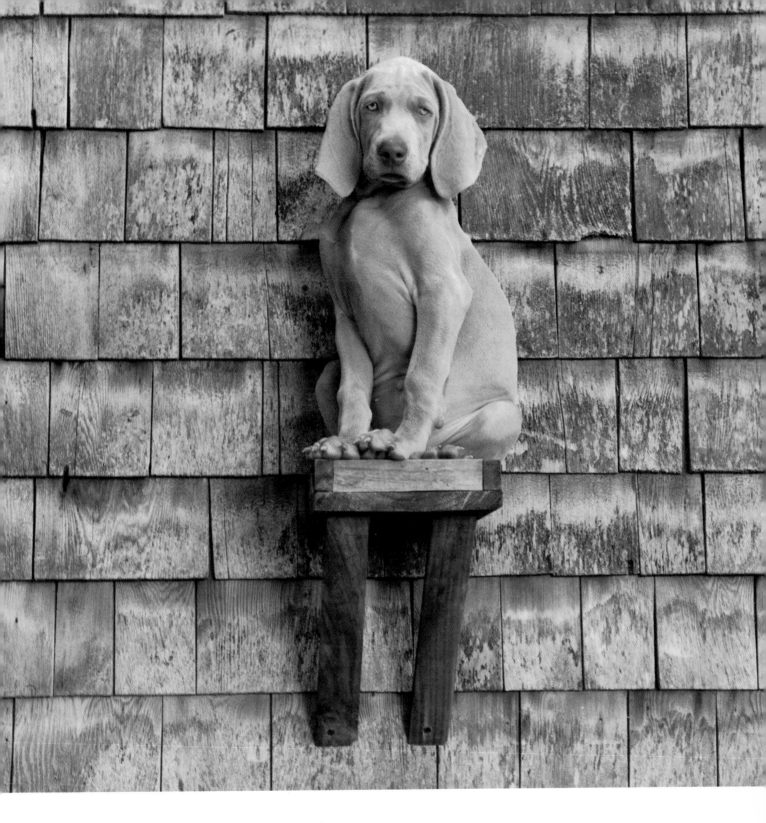

Pup Prop

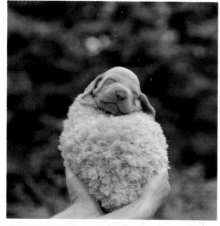

Dream Puff

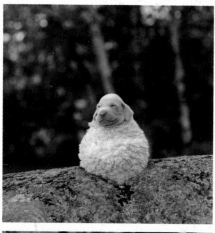

Puddie

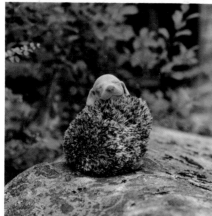

Lichen

Posted

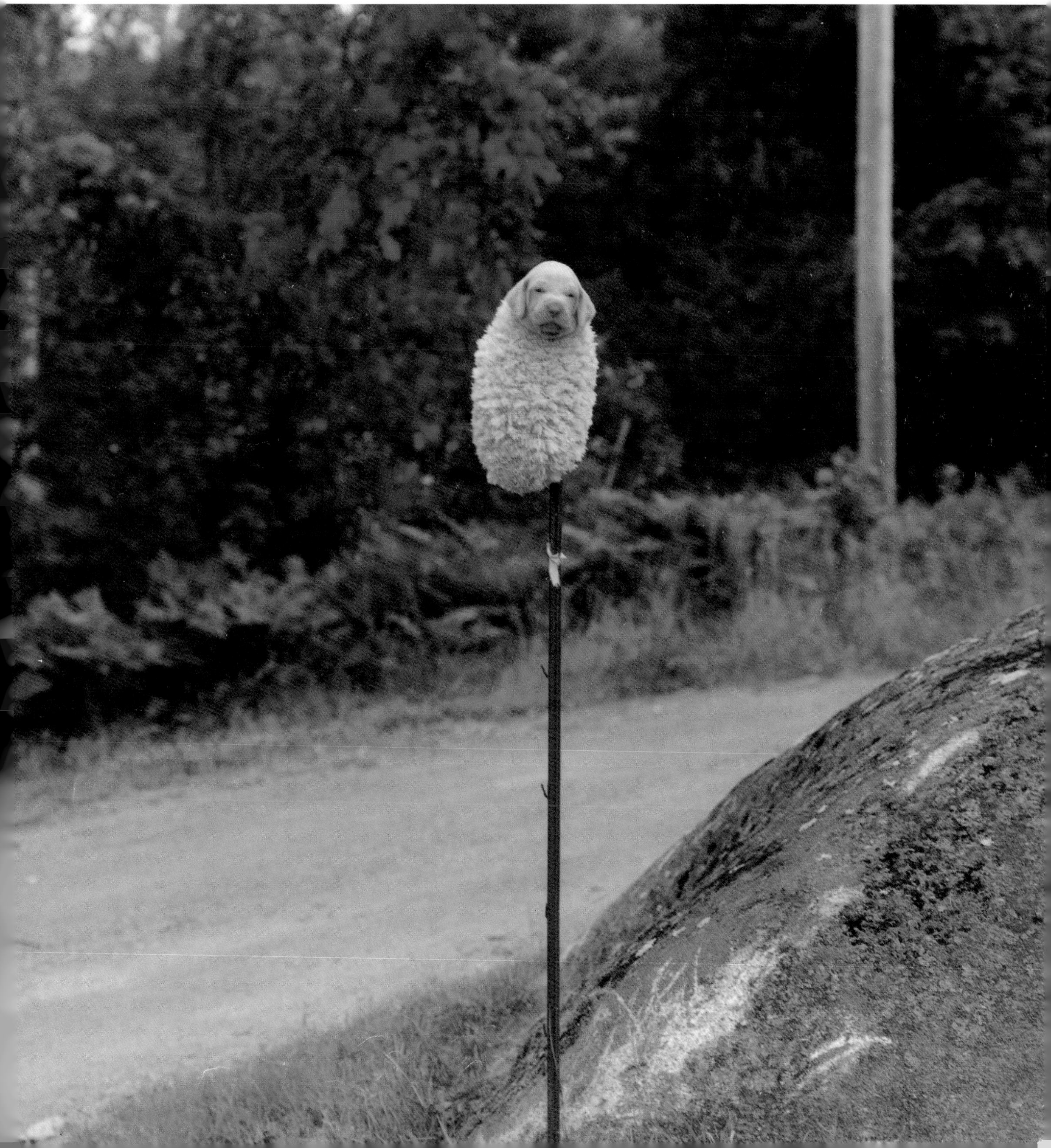

Young Chundo

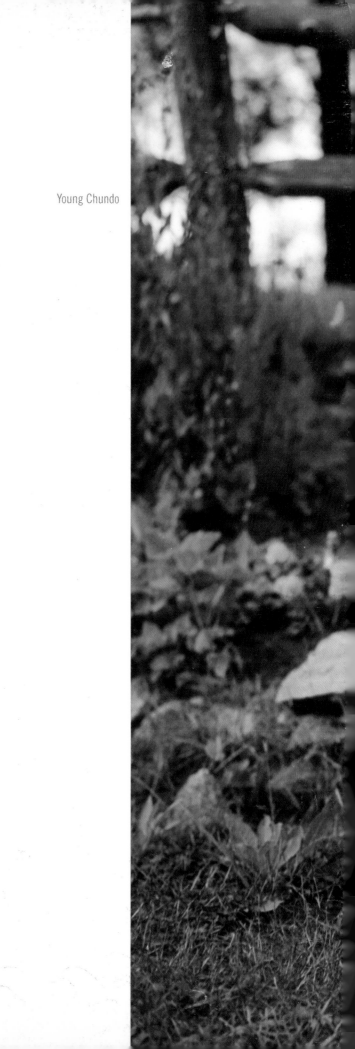

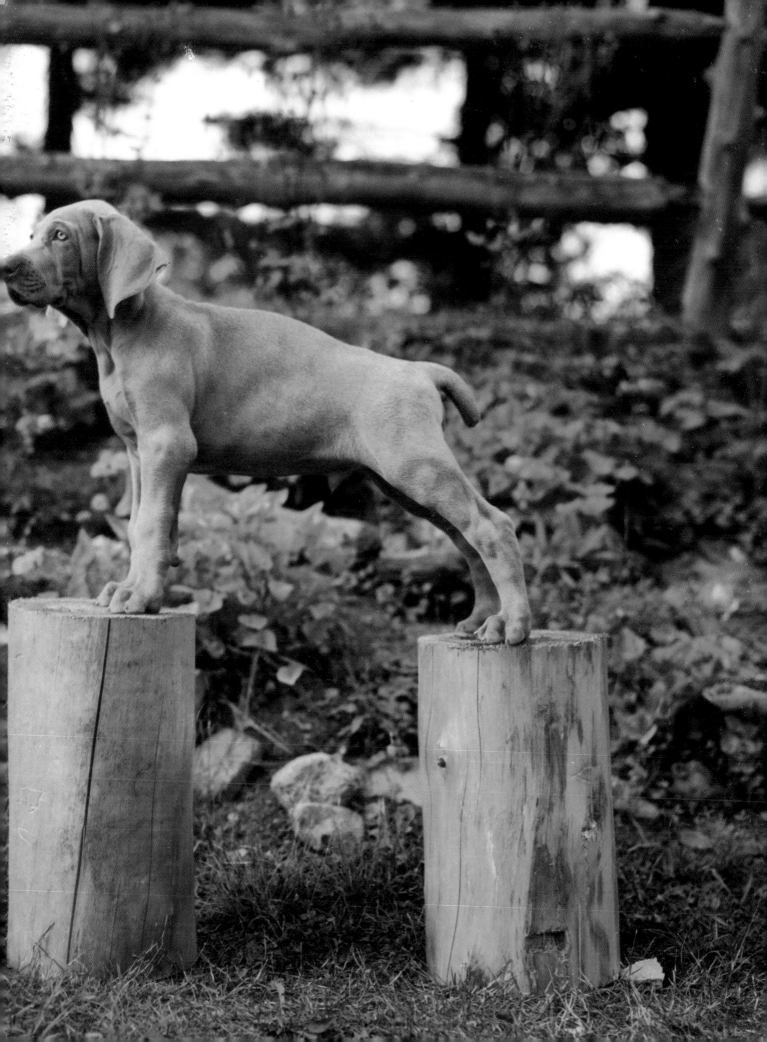

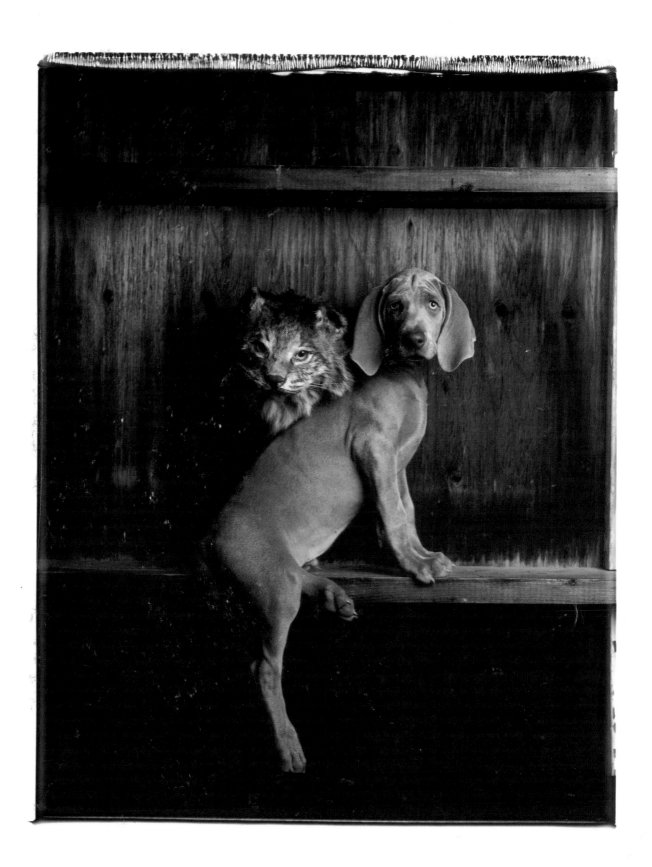

Cat Back

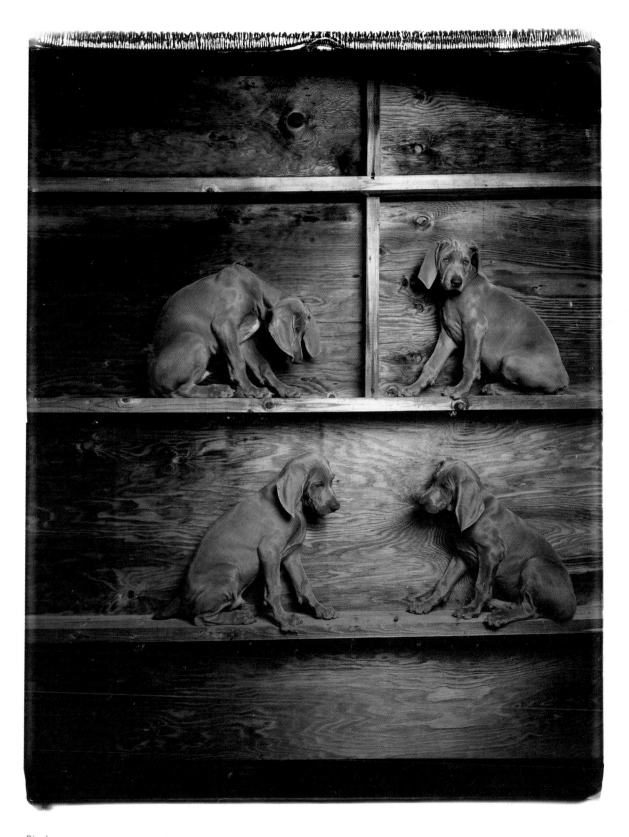

Display

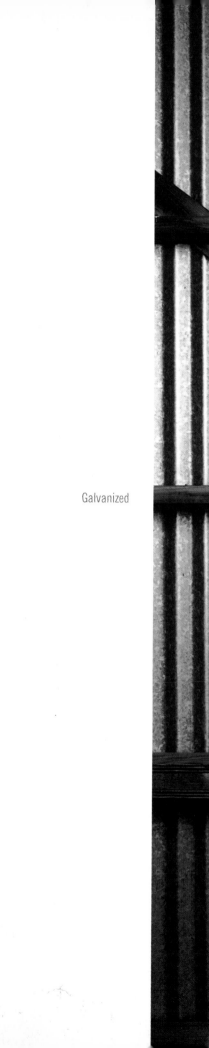

Galvanized

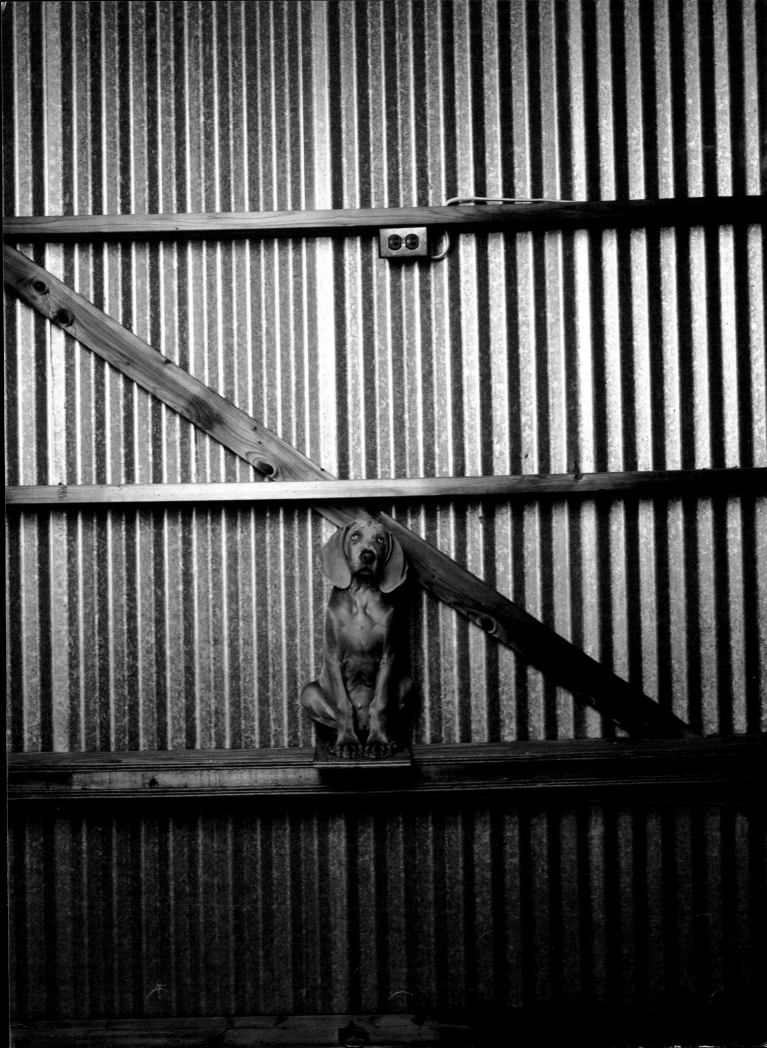

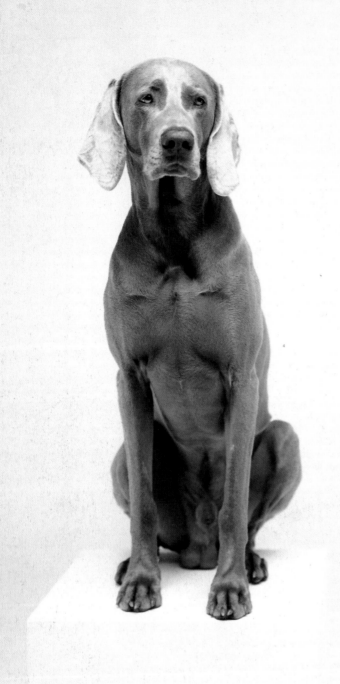
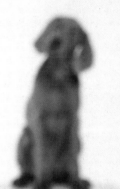

Man Ray, Fay, Crooky, Batty, Chundo,

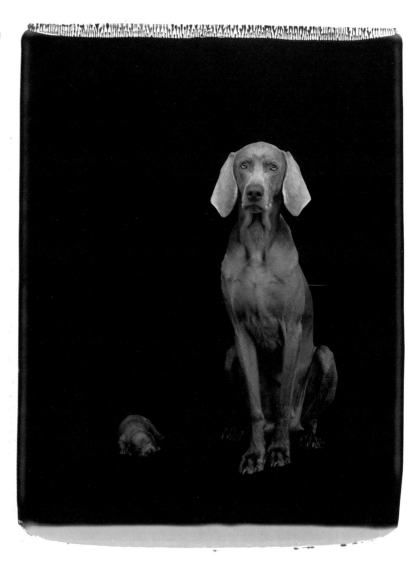

and now Chip.

There have been

three litters since

Fay's first family.

Crooky was the next to give birth. Her first litter, unplanned, delivered a cornucopia of eleven mixed Labrador weimaraners.

The second was less romantic, an arranged marriage in June of 1993 with a weimaraner named Champion Grayshire Valient von Reiteralm (also known as Val). This resulted in a litter of six gray puppies. Crooky was a good mother, more at ease with her condition than Fay had been. She took it all in stride. I enjoyed photographing her puppies. It was liberating not having to choose one puppy to keep. Crooky's offspring

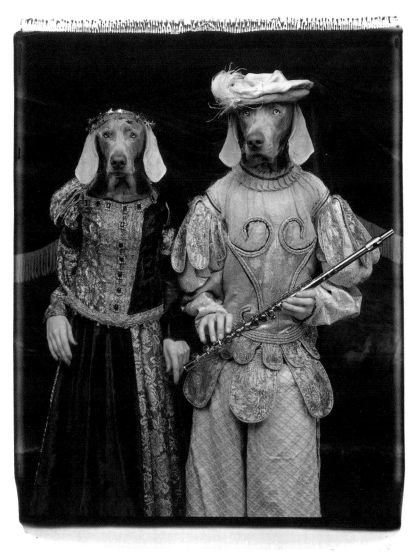

The Magic Flute
(Battina and Chip)

The big dogs showed the youngsters the way to enlightened posing.

live in New York, Connecticut, Rhode Island, Massachusetts, and Maine and I rarely see them, but Dave, her owner, keeps in touch. They are all doing fine and are all large dogs, which is surprising since Crooky is petite. My theory is that Dave made her sleep on a very small dog bed. I have no idea if this is true.

Choosing a husband for Batty was an interesting process. Every male weimaraner that happened by got my attention. *"Hi, what's your name?"* Never mind...too tall. *"Hi, who are you?"* No, too pointy in the snout...or something. Then one day I met him. He was jumping over a fence, a fence made to be jumped over by a dog.

Battina became
serious. In effect,
she became Fay.

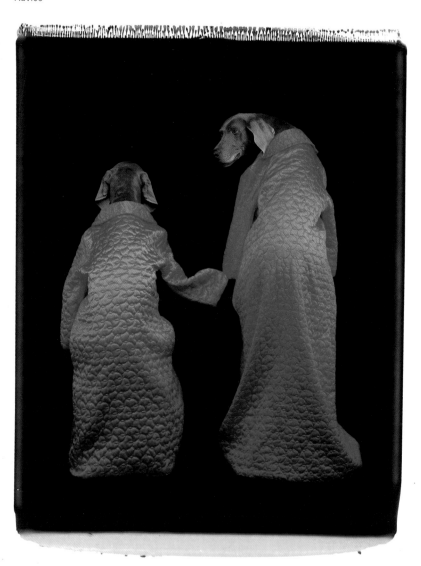

After he jumped, he would fetch a parcel, one of three, and jump back over the fence to return it to his master. He looked great. *"Hi. What's his name?" "Ferdinand." "Batty, say hello to Ferdinand. He's a good boy."*

Batty gave birth to a litter of four, all boys. This time I was well prepared. By week six I had Virginia Alexander's recently published book, *Weimaraner Ways*, open to the appropriate section and had Batty's whelping box and heat lamp all set up in the bedroom. I had the vet's phone numbers posted, as well as Virginia's. It turned out we needed them all.

On May 19, 1995, Batty went into labor, right on schedule. The first puppy arrived headfirst without a sac, and as far as I could tell, not breathing. After repeated swings, rubs, and pinches got no response, I called the vet. *"Keep trying."* I gave up and passed the puppy in a towel over to my wife, Christine, who kept rubbing determinedly. Batty watched anxiously. Fay looked concerned. After ten minutes we heard a peep. Christine gave the puppy to Batty, and he began to nurse. A miracle. The next two boys arrived without a hitch, but then trouble— a girl born in the sac but covered in meconium (black goo).

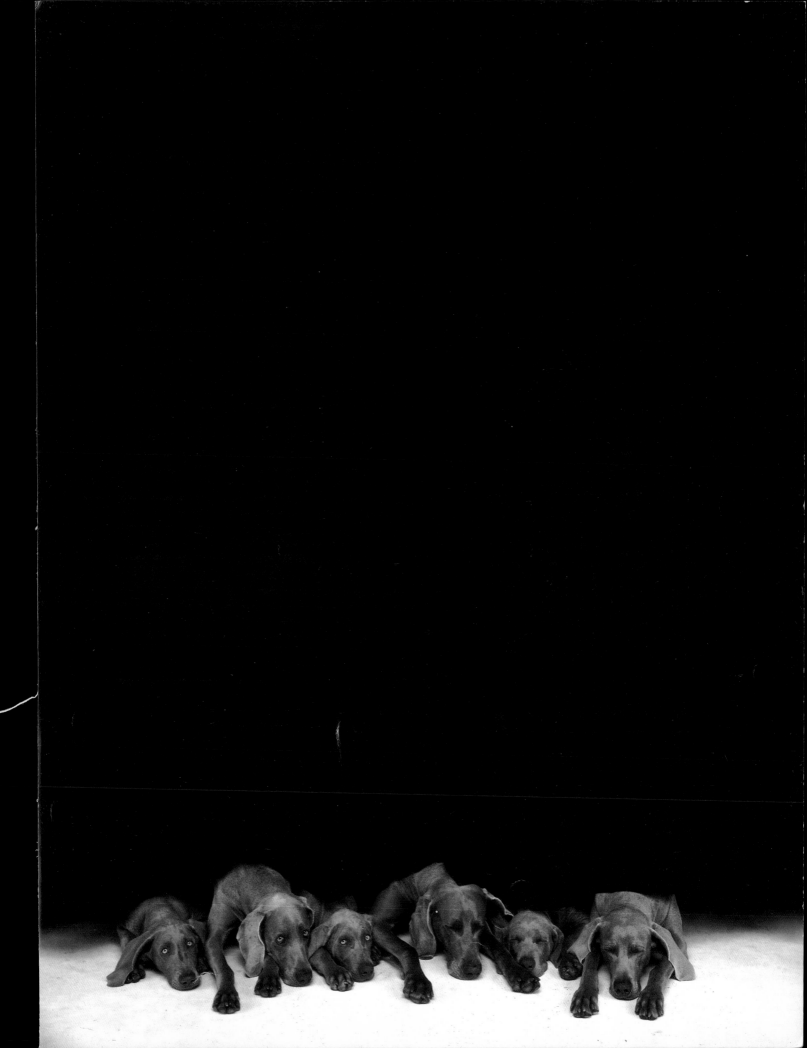

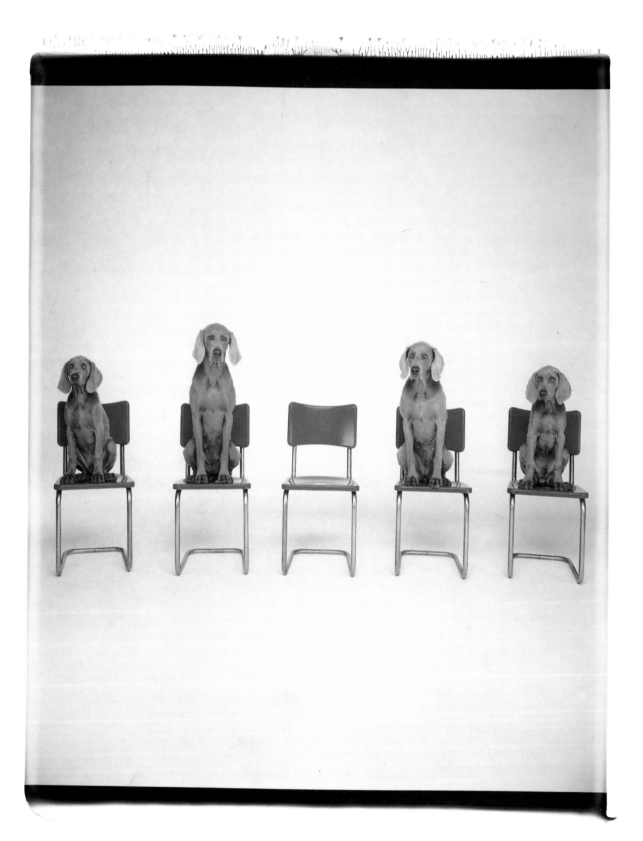

Roll Call

Christine, flush with success from the first one, worked furiously but to no avail. Sadly, after more than thirty minutes of frantic rubbing, she gave up. We waited hours for the next puppy, whose presence we were practically certain of from a sonogram. Finally, we took Batty to Dr. Greene, who was able to deliver the final one. We had given all the puppies collars of different colors in order to tell them apart, and this puppy was given a green collar and a name: Dr. Green.

Three weeks after Batty's litter was born, Fay became ill. She had leukemia. This was hard to believe and impossible to accept. Fay was only ten years old, and other than having a terminal illness, she was in perfect health. Fay seemed so strong that even the fraction of a percent of a chance that chemotherapy would work seemed like a sure thing at the time. But nothing worked, no amount of medicine or squeaky toys or sleeping with Fay at the vet. Within two weeks Fay died.

When Fay became sick, Batty began to change. At first she was disoriented. She had always looked to Fay for cues. After we found out about Fay's illness, Fay came home to spend the weekend with us, and during that time she seemed to explain things to Battina. Battina began to inhabit places only occupied by Fay in the past, places that Batty had never dared venture: under my desk, "Fay's" chair, Christine's side of the bed. Battina became serious. In effect, she became Fay.

Even though it was difficult to return to Maine that summer without Fay, we did. I was relieved to have Batty's four new puppies to keep me busy and was anxious to work with them. We arranged two shoots with the 20 x 24 Polaroid camera that summer—one in Maine and one back in New York. The big dogs showed the youngsters the way to enlightened posing just as Batty, too, had learned to pose from Fay. Even the wild-eyed ones, like Crooky, performed well when they all worked together.

Chip no longer fits into his Little Jack Horner outfit.

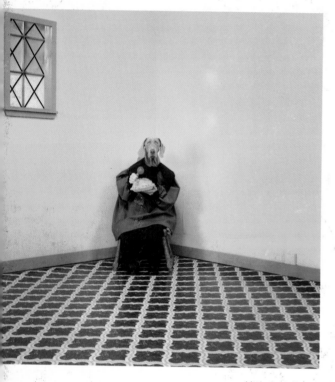

Little Jack Horner

Chip, the one Christine had resurrected, was the most mellow and certainly the easiest to work with. He was relaxed like Batty yet inquisitive and alert. He had a large, handsome head like his father. I had first thought Dr. Green the most photo-genic, but now I was zooming in on Chip. He loved being photographed, and his eyes lit up the picture like no other. I fell in love with him as I had with Fay and Batty before.

Man Ray, Fay, Crooky, Batty, Chundo, and now Chip. Dogs grow old at an almost perceivable rate, and the time when they are puppies soars by the quickest. By the time I have an idea, they have outgrown it. Better act fast. Chip is already on his way to maturity. At this writing, he is just over one year old. Unlike wise, stoic Man Ray and serious, eager Chundo, Chip is endearingly juvenile, exuding adolescence. He no longer fits into his Little Jack Horner outfit, nor would he appear thin enough to wear the jacket and trousers of lean Jack Sprat, roles he played just a few months ago. He and Uncle Chundo are great together. Some of my favorite recent pictures feature them. Boy versus Man. Unlike the other dogs, Chip has no interest in a ball (among weimaraners an almost universal object of desire), so when working, I will have to find new methods to get his attention. Right now he just sits there gazing out beyond the lens of the big camera in sublime non-anticipation.

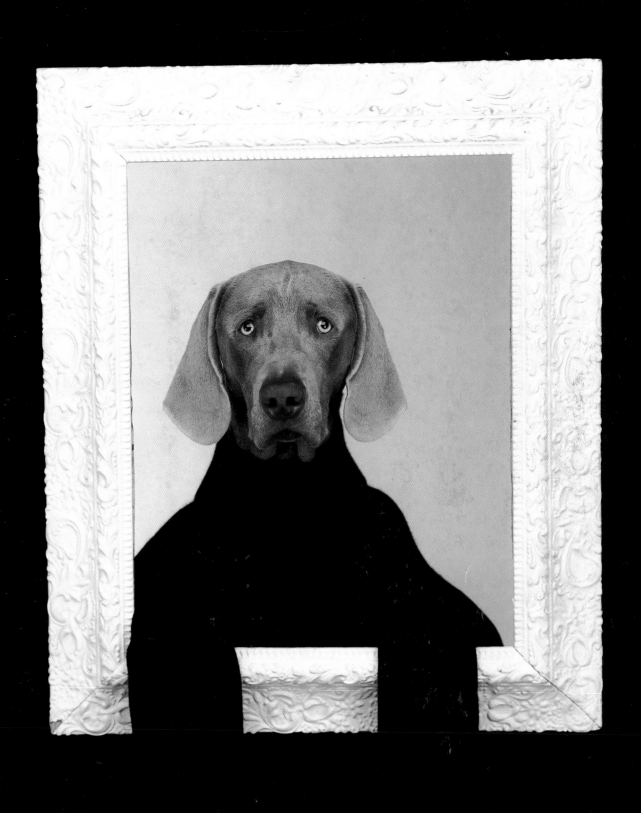

Printed in the United States of America.

First Edition
10 9 8 7 6 5 4 3 2

Library of Congress
Cataloging-in-Publication Data
Wegman, William.
[Puppies]
William Wegman's puppies/William
Wegman.—1st ed.
          p.   cm.
Summary: A photo essay presenting an
overview of the birth and upbringing of
William Wegman's famous Weimaraners.
ISBN 0-7868-0320-7 (trade)
1. Weimaraners (Dogs)—Infancy
—Juvenile literature.
2. Photography of dogs—Juvenile
literature.
[1. Weimaraners (Dogs) 2. Dogs.]
I. Title II. Title: Puppies.
SF429.W33W44   1997
636.752—DC21
96-54626

Design: Drenttel Doyle Partners
This Book is set in Trade Gothic and Scala.

Acknowledgments

Mary Alberti, Virginia Alexander, Stan
Bartash, Andrea Beeman, Jason Burch,
Christine Burgin, Adam Clemens, Patsy
Desmond, Dr. Peter Dingley, Lorraine
Dingley, Stephen Doyle, Drenttel Doyle
Partners, Alexandra Edwards, Stacy
Fischer, Dr. Richard Greene, Julie
Hindley, Arnaldo Hernandez, Barbara
Jacobs, Eric Jeffreys, Trisha Krauss,
Azan Kung, Asia Linn, Lisa Martin,
Peter MacGill, Dave McMillan, Pace
Wildenstein MacGill Gallery, Carline
Rankine, Howard Reeves, John Reuter,
Terry Rozo, Dale Rubin, Chris Schiavo,
Bridget Shields, Katleen Sterck,
Tracy Storer, John Slyce, Gary Tooth,
Jeanette Ward, Gayle Wegman, Pam
Wegman, and Fran York.